This story is dedicated to everyone on the autistic spectrum.

I0450934

Table of Contents

THE DISCARDED KNIGHT

By
Andrew Johnston

The Discarded Knight
First Edition

Chapter 1

Water roared into the drain, turning into a repetitive thudding once the stopper plugged its escape. Countless droplets thundered against the tub's porcelain in random patterns. Alfred wanted desperately to cover his ears. His hands rose slightly from his rocking horse, but the thought of letting go was as frightening as the water filling the tub. The wooden horse rocked back and forth on the ornately stitched rug at the room's center. Sweat ran down his cheeks as he clenched his teeth and looked at the floor again. Thoughts of the brave knights leaping from their horses in Elsa's stories sounded exciting. Yet he was no knight, and his socks were slippery, unlike the sturdy boots a knight wore to battle.

Elsa hummed in her graceful way, the rhythm drifting from the loo to his ears and easing the prickling up and down his back. The tune was something that always made him smile no matter what the day or evening brought.

"It's almost filled, Alfred," she said. Her words eased his nerves unlike the hurried ticks from his clock above his bed.

Despite not yet being able to tell time, Alfred sensed his bedtime was close. Minutes passed before the rushing water slowed, though to him it was still deafening. His hands searched for a way to gain control of the brightly painted horse. He wanted desperately to be like the knights from Elsa's stories.

Those knights, though, didn't have their horses' reins painted on. His nerves were raw now, as raw as they would get from London's great clock tower chiming every hour on the hour. The tower was many blocks away, but to him the tower could stand to be much, much farther. Easing his little foot down, the chances of falling doubled. So, he pulled it back, thrusting it into one of the horse's leather stirrups.

"Esa! Esa!" he cried, trying to call her from the loo.

When her head popped up in the doorway, he swallowed his fear and put on a brave face at the sight of her grin. "The water is to your liking, my little knight!"

The name she often called him always made him to want to do things on his own. After she gave him a wave, her rosy, red lips turned away and she returned to filling the tub. Now it was more important than even a bath or bedtime for him to be brave. Alfred did not want to let her down.

He reached again, the toe of his sock wrinkling against the rug as the tips of his fingers dug into the horse's wooden mane. The balls of his toes were almost planted when—duuuum, duuum, dum, dum. With the first chime, his left leg gave with fright, and then his right. Alfred wailed. The click of Elsa's heels overwhelmed the thud his head made.

"Alfred, what happened?" She knelt beside him. Her face was red and panicked like his.

The door swung open to reveal his mother just as his arm and head began to throb.

"What has happened to my son?" Josephine's violet nightgown shifted and danced, tightening when she knelt short of his head. "He is only of age five! Where were you?" she asked Elsa.

Alfred's free hand reached for Elsa, but his mother picked him up instead. Elsa tried to explain. The clock tower's chiming ended, only to bring heavy footfalls from outside the room.

"What on earth is all this noise?" His father's voice boomed in its commanding fashion from the hallway.

"She was not watching him, Charles," Josephine cried.

He entered, looming over Alfred as a sneer twisted his lips. Alfred buried his face in his mother's chest. Elsa whimpered, facing his father, trying to explain again. She pressed her hands together and peered up at him, pleading still, but Charles silenced her with a wave of his hand.

"Young lady, you had best tell me our city's clock tower isn't to blame for this." Charles clenched his teeth, bristling his finely trimmed beard just as Alfred peeked up.

Alfred watched his father press the black of his polished shoes into the rug. His mind raced as his mother's hand stroked his head. The thought of what might happen made him shudder. Charles focused his unyielding green eyes on Elsa. Alfred sniffed, trying to smile once Elsa's eyes rested on him.

"I was drawing him a bath, sir," said Elsa, tears easing down her cheeks. "I knew he liked to ride horses like the knights in the tourneys and—"

"Filling my son's head with fairy tales is not what I pay you for." Charles motioned with a finger callused from years at his slaughterhouses. "Come. We shall speak of this further in my study."

Elsa followed Charles out of the room. Alfred reached for her, not wanting her to leave him. Her hands shook in rhythm with his as he reached and tugged away from his mother.

"Esa? Esa, where you going?" His eyes blurred from more tears, smearing her movements. The door whined the closer it came to closing. "Where?" he wailed as Elsa's rosy, red lips gave him one last smile.

"Pleasant dreams, my little knight."

Alfred continued to cry while his mother undressed him. Soon he found himself up high again, making him cover his eyes. After falling from the slow rocking horse, any height was like a mountain. The water drank in his fear with its warmth when she eased him in and began to wash his back.

"Does your arm still hurt?"

He winced when she stroked it with the washcloth.

"No." Alfred pulled it away, pretending her fingers pressing through soap and cloth didn't make it worse. "Where es Esa?"

Alfred moved from the tub's edge. Water sloshed like he was a steamer plowing up the English Channel. Waves splash over the white tub and clattered upon the floor. He didn't know where the study was or how to get there. The nursery and Elsa's stories framed the life that was his. Now that frame gaped like a mouth without words, thanks to Elsa not being around to speak them. Her stories made the emptiness of his room easier to manage once alone in bed.

"Your father has taken her to have a private word."

"What es privat' wor'?"

Josephine closed her eyes for a moment and then said, "It's 'private word." She corrected. "I know you are young, but you must learn to speak properly."

"What a private wor'?"

Her lips curled up when he said it. Alfred wished she wouldn't get so mad when he spoke. At present, he wasn't worried so much about how he spoke but for the one friend missing from the bedtime fast approaching. His mother would always come and kiss him good night, but she didn't know any stories. Splash went his hand in the water. Josephine moved to the side, bumping her shoulder on the sink. The violet of her nightgown became a deep purple from the water.

"And you will act like a proper child as well!"

An unseen grip to his good arm joined a rag lathered in soap to his lips, muffling his cries, each one asking for Elsa and that her little knight needed her. Yet like the dragon of so many of Elsa's stories, Alfred's mother proved to be mighty.

Pulling and pulling, he could not fight her with such small hands, arms, and legs. They did not compare to the boys he saw from his window that he wanted to meet. That and his mother was not the real dragon to face. That dragon held Elsa down in a place far from his room, a place Alfred had never been to, where another creature dwelled, a *private word*.

The bath was soon replaced by towels, followed by a fresh pair of new pajamas. They were itchy, making him miss the soft ones Elsa had made. Their red and blue stripes forced him to close his eyes when his room's oil sconces shined through their fabric.

"I don't like these, Mum," he said. "They're not the ones Esa—"

"I know you *shall* like them. They are new, and I only just purchased them from the afternoon's errands."

She adjusted them while Alfred tightened his lips like a shield against her piercing words.

"Do not look at me in such a way." She snapped. "Your old ones had holes and a queer smell."

The bed sheets were strange in the newer clothes. The sleeves were too big, tangling as she tucked the blanket around him. He twisted and tugged until his hands and arms were over the top. His eyes narrowed and rolled from the kiss she gave him. The story that followed the nightly annoyance was still missing like his friend. Alfred peered up and over the covers to the door, ignoring the low hiss of the oil lamps being turned down.

"Will Esa be comin' back?" he whispered before the door swallowed his mother in the hall's dim throat. "She hasn't told me a story yet."

Alfred pulled at the covers as Josephine looked at him with a sad face. He could tell there would be no story, but the reassurance was something he always needed.

"Neither Elsa nor I shall be telling you any stories, my son. You can face the night without one, as a growing boy must do." She pulled the door until only her nose and brown eyes showed in the flickering light. "Good night."

Click went the door as did his mind, trying to recall every story Elsa had ever told. When she finished a new one, he would tug at her hand for an old one before she stood. The ones of the tourneys in the shadow of a great mountain among a crowd of cheering villagers were the best. Shutting his eyes, he mouthed every detail he remembered until his lips ceased their movement.

The crowd roared, waving tiny flags of many colors. Some were green, yellow, red, or blue, displaying beasts ready to face ones from faraway places. One knight readied himself below an eagle with a white head on a red, white, and blue banner. Another knight did the same, with a bear of black and white upon a red flag.

Alfred sat atop a cushioned chair within a four-columned viewing stand. Horse hooves stomped at the already grassless lists, kicking up dust. He gripped the cushion, waiting for the joust to begin. The cushion's smooth fabrics felt almost real with every dream. Whatever itch there had been from the new pajamas was replaced by the soft silks of his gray doublet.

Boys a few years older than him ran out with colorfully painted lances. One he thought for a moment was missing an eye. Alfred noticed as the boy hoisted the lance mouthing something in his direction that seemed strange to say at a tourney. *"Help us."*

The boy returned to raising the lance, stumbling a bit from the weapon's weight and length. The lance itself was nearly three times the boy's height. He released it to the mounted knight, breathing easy, and then disappeared into the crowd. Alfred shrugged, clapping once both knights slammed their visors shut, bouncing on his cushion. He had the viewing stand all to himself until a floorboard creaked.

Slender fingers rested softly on his little shoulders. Looking up, there she was, except her blonde hair was not in a bun like usual but resting on her shoulders. Elsa's smile was somewhat dimmer than usual once she joined him in the seat beside him.

"Esa." He laughed, admiring her gray-sleeved dress.

Trumpets sounded as she pressed her attention upon the two knights now at full gallop. Alfred could not turn his eyes toward the armored men. She was there, and neither his father nor a private word could keep her from him. A crack followed by a panicking horse broke his focus. The crowd roared as the knight with the bear shield fell to the ground. He clapped loudly as Elsa did. The floor creaked again, but Alfred was so focused on his friend's excitement that he didn't pay it any mind. Another pair of hands gripped his shoulders. They were coarse and thick, just like the words being whispered in his ear.

"Wake up." The voice urged. "Your lessons will be starting soon. As shall the road to becoming a man, and a man is never late."

The coarse hands became scaly and the fingertips black claws. Alfred looked up to see smoke hiding the face the tightening hands belonged to. Glowing green eyes peered through the smoke as Alfred cried out, "Esa! Esa!"

But his friend was gone when the smoke filled the viewing stand. All he could see were glowing green eyes. The familiar smell of dried blood pinched his nose. Alfred squirmed and twisted, gagging while his hands reached and clawed. The seat's velvet was soft and sleek, helping his bum to the edge. The claws dug deeper, yanking him back into the smoke.

Alfred's eyes shot open, focusing squarely upon his father.

"Your mother shall be in shortly." Charles stood up straight, his eyes a brighter green than usual, almost glowing before he made his way to the door. But when the door was almost shut, his eyes were normal again after Alfred had rubbed his own. "Do us both a common courtesy and don't speak of fairy tales. A Richards keeps to his studies."

The new pajamas were replaced by new clothes. They fit better, yet Alfred still preferred his old ones.

"The tutor will be here in an hour," Josephine said after properly tying his tie and opening the door. "Let us head down to the dining room. After we finish breakfast, your tutor will meet you in the study."

Seconds after her mentioning the study, Alfred's eyes lit up. He moved quickly through the door, a smile on his face, ready to save his friend. His polished black shoes stopped short of the steps. His nose was greeted by the smell of cooking bacon. Alfred knew the smell well though he had always enjoyed its peppery crunch from within his room. It was the stairs separating him from the smell and his friend. He had never been down them, nor had he ever seen much of the house. Neither the maid nor Elsa nor even his mother had allowed him out his room until now. Once, he'd tried to turn the doorknob. It had barely moved, only clicked, making him giggle. He'd done it repeatedly until his father had put a stop to it.

"Come now," said his mother, urging him gently with a hand to his shoulder. "Your breakfast will be cold."

Alfred could sense the impatience in her voice while his eyes were mesmerized by the number of steps.

"Carry me down." He looked up at her, finding the same look she had given him last night.

"I shall be thankful for your lessons," she said. "It will teach you to speak as I have said, properly."

Her hand nudged him toward the railing. His hand gripped at a rung almost thin enough for his little hand to wrap around. The bacon smell grew stronger as did his wish to save Elsa. His foot shook the lower it went from where the carpet ended. He pulled it up just short of the wood below.

Josephine made an impatient sound under her breath almost like the horses in his dream.

"Please, Mum," said Alfred. His lips trembled and fingers shook. "I can't do it me self. It's too high."

He wanted to save his friend, he wanted the bacon, and though he wanted to be brave, the stairs were frightening. Alfred needed his mother to be the one to take him there. She crossed her arms when he took a step back from the edge and toward her. He looked at her with strained eyes, but her face remained cold, emotionless.

"I don't want to fall again."

"I wish for you to be educated and sound so."

He reached up to her, peering back to the steps and then back up to her. Redness peeked from under the sleeve of his injured arm. His mother eyed it and sighed.

"Until you are bigger, I shall, Alfred."

She raised him into her arms, taking the steps with caution. His wish to save Elsa numbed the fear of being so high, but only for a tiny bit. His shoes tapped the fine, finished wood near the front door. The bacon smell intensified to his right, yet Elsa's rescue dried the watering of his mouth.

"I want to go to da study."

"Not before you have had breakfast." Josephine pointed to a clock above the door. "Your lessons are in forty minutes."

"But I want to..."

Josephine urged his shoulder, pointing to a plate atop a long table in a larger room than any he had ever seen. Plantlike patterns formed the back of four chairs at each of its sides. Alfred looked over his shoulder, thinking the closed door led to the study.

"To the dining room with haste, please. Your tutor will be arriving shortly."

He did not want her to become angrier than she already was. And his stomach had been growling from the moment they left his room. Alfred took one last look at the shut door and then waddled to the table. The chair was just low enough for him to reach. With three great hops, Alfred almost made it up on the third try only to feel his mother lift him into the seat.

The hot peppery crunch he'd expected was a cold blandness. He swallowed, making a face to fight the taste. His mother sat to his left taking short, quick sips from her tea, seeming to compete with the quick bites he made at his toast. A crunch of the last bite finished the race. Milk finished off what lingered behind his lips. Slamming the glass on the table, he focused down at the floor. Alfred tried to ease himself down as quickly as possible. He slammed his eyes shut. Hearing his mother take a final sip, both hands let go of the chair. Shoes scraped the rug, giving way for his bottom to plop hard and fast to the floor. He planted his hands uneasily and he tried to stand up. Josephine rushed his side, growing panic overcoming her face. He straightened his lips, stiffened his brow, and gave her a nod. His mother sided pressing her hand to her chest. His wish to prove braver than last night worked, but now his bottom hurt.

The pain did not matter, and when he peered back at the chair, neither did the fall. All that mattered was Elsa. A tiny jingle went off as he passed the front door with his mother close behind. Another woman's voice joined his mother's when the door opened. It was brisk and light like his feet as they carried him to the study.

"Esa!" he yelled, pushing open the door.

Books lined the walls, a large desk stood straight ahead, and big, fierce animal heads roared from above. Taking a step back, he wasn't sure if they would attack or not.

"Good morning, Alfred."

Alfred spun, trying to ignore the fearsome glares of the animals. The woman looked like Elsa, young and thin, yet her hair was brown, and she had a mole below her left eye that he could not stop staring at.

"Shall we begin?" She closed the door, setting a stack of books on the low table to her right. "My name is Gwen, and your mother says I am to teach you proper English."

"Where is Esa?" Alfred looked around again. The animal heads were the only things around besides him and the tutor. And her mole stuck out like a pointing finger. "Does da priv word got her, or Father?"

Gwen looked at him, shaking her head as he spoke. "Yes," she said, "we most certainly have much work ahead. Come, let us begin, shall we?"

She inched slowly past the table, keeping her eyes on him, and then she sank into the couch's leather. Alfred took a short step, resting fingers on the table's edge. She placed a book upon the table and slid to him, open it in one swift motion. And when he looked down, her mole didn't stick out as much. Gwen was more like Elsa than he'd thought. The page of the book revealed a knight, except he was not like the ones Alfred knew. The knight sported a mustache while fighting a windmill. Alfred gulped and froze, remembering what his father had said.

"I'm not supposed to talk 'bout fairy tales." He closed the book. The cover was red with the knight on a white horse. "Father said I must stick to me studies."

Gwen opened the book.

"I think your father and mother want what is in your best interests." She flipped to the first page, giving him a small smile. "This is for children, Alfred, and when you can say and read all the words in it. Then we will move on to other studies."

Scanning the words, her lips sounded them out faster than his mind could understand at first. His thoughts were still on Elsa, where she was or if she was coming back. It didn't seem so as the days passed. The words became a little bit easier to read with each lesson, yet when the clock tower chimed, it not only bothered him but also gave a reminder. And every time he was carried to his room for bed, his mother would make him wear the itchy, brightly colored pajamas.

Alfred stared at the ceiling, teary-eyed one night, asking if it had been his fault. Eventually, after many more nights, he believed there was no other reason she was still not back. Even when his dreams brought him back to the arena again and again, he couldn't find her, and the stands were empty with each dream. The mountain loomed ahead of him, shading the aged wood of the arena. A breeze ran across his face like water over a shallow riverbed. It was cold, making Alfred wonder how it could be. He remembered every story was accompanied by the summer season. But that did not make him blame himself any less for his friend being gone.

"I'll neva be brave to want somethin' again."

Just short of noon the next morning Gwen clapped when he finished a full sentence. He saw how happy she was and grabbed his pencil. He pretended to be the knight upon the book's cover. Gwen told him a knight would need his lunch, so he ran out the door.

Alfred's father was coming from the dining room, his eyes focused on a newspaper article. Swinging and lunging, the two almost collided, forcing his father to lose his balance. The fall sent Charles's pocket watch from his waist jacket pocket. It smashed against a wall as Charles landed against the stairs. He rose, regaining his balance and snatched up the newspaper. Alfred backed away from his father's anger until he bumped into the coatrack. An open palm raised, and his father's hand swung downward.

Chapter 2

A sniff and a stretching turn reminded Alfred he had fallen asleep with a book on his chest. The book fell, knocking over a stack he had read and never put away, ranging from a book on fixing pocket watches to one called *Le Compte de Monte-Cristo*. Light from the early morning sun streamed through the window, almost reaching the toppled books. His climb from the bed was less daunting now that he was older, though he was still quite short. Even now at seventeen, his mother and father loomed over him.

Alfred buttoned each button in quick succession and tucked his shirt in, remembering the conversation of yesterday. An idea had come to his mind while he'd been waiting for Gwen. She was running late that morning from another student's session. Just before starting their speech lesson, he'd asked her.

"Are we friends, even though you're my teacher and all?"

"Yes, I consider all of my students my friends." She'd smiled, giving his hand a pat.

Alfred was glad to have her as one, but after she'd left, the same loneliness crept up his back. Its only repellent had been the books he read, inviting their characters to keep him company. Rubbing his eyes and forehead, Alfred passed the toppled pile beside the other neat stacks. He was tired of the same characters. Their lives were what he wanted to live, not dream, or read about.

Dallying toward the stairs, his eyes closed for what felt like the millionth time. The stairs disappeared into the already dim stairwell. Its only light came from the low burning oil sconces and the front door's window. The clicking of the maid's heels and the ruffle of his father's newspaper greeted him from four steps up. Every trip was also faster since he counted the steps for assurance.

Across from his father, Alfred hopped onto his usual seat near the dining room entrance. The question was at the middle of his tongue when both received their plates. Charles was in his usual black waistcoat, sporting cufflinks containing the Richards crest. The crest possessed a dragon that's head, and neck were a sort of 'R' shape. The dragon's jaws and its scales were a polished gold. One cufflink made a ting against a plate when Charles took a slice of bacon. It was now or many more silent breakfasts to come. Alfred cleared his throat.

"Father, I was wonderin.'" His eyes narrowed to his plate.

A quick crunch and swallow answered him first.

"You were wondering what? I must leave for work soon, and I am never late." Charles wiped a bit of bacon grease from his lips. "It is surprising to see you have adopted that finally. Breakfast should always be when the day is at its youngest."

"I was..." The words fought through Alfred's trembling lips. "I was wondering if I could go to school with other kids."

There was a slight snicker in response. Immediately his mind raced when it rose to a chuckle, subsiding ever so slowly.

"Why now? We tried to make you go when you were six." Charles folded the newspaper in his lap, resting it on the table.

His amusement turned to a glare as he finished a small cup of tea. "You complained the entire time of the other children mocking you."

"They made fun me being little and how I always look—"

"And you wish to face that again?" Charles peeked at his pocket watch, sliding it back into his waist pocket. "I shall spare us the trouble of that again and my being late. The answer is no."

"But, Father, I am so lonely, and I have not left the house in..."

"There is sound reasoning behind it," Charles said. "You will have to prove you can manage yourself amongst others."

Alfred looked up from his plate as his father rose. Grabbing his coat and buttoning it, Charles made his way to the door. His top hat made a thud against the coatrack's balled nob. The door soon opened, ready to close until Charles made one final demand.

"Until you can do so, you will be schooled here and remain indoors." Charles securely fitted his gloves, adding, "You can't even keep eye contact with your own father. How does one win any friends if one does not look at them?"

The door slammed, making Alfred jump a little.

"How can I anyway?" he mumbled as he lowered himself from the chair. "I don't see anybody other than Gwen, the maids, Mum, an' you."

A few steps later he was in the study. The fearsome animal heads along the walls had become a part of his routine. After the second day he'd had with Gwen, he realized they weren't going to eat him. The hour at its mid, and his tutor wouldn't arrive until seven. His every thought was focused on his father's last words. As he waited, he readied all that his lessons required, arranging the pencils and papers, and pulling a book from the shelf. He shrugged and decided it was worth reading a third time.

How he could prove himself cycled over and over until his mother entered. Alfred looked straight at her, not breaking eye contact as she spoke.

"Well." Her eyes perked open. He tried not to look away, unable to understand why she was so sluggish of late. "Are you ready for your final lesson with Gwen?"

The straining of his eyes lessoned falling to ground as his mouth gaped. Her announcement brought his attempt at improving himself to a screeching halt.

"What? Why it would be her las' day?" His lips trembled the closer he moved to her. "I talk...I mean, I speak much better than I did."

A sudden change to things was not what he needed now. Adding to his distress was the way his mother's lips always stiffened when he spoke.

"I will admit that you have improved dramatically," she said. "However, you are no longer a child, and you must move on to—"

"Why? Why must I or anythin' move on?" His face bunched with rage as hers turned to jelly, forcing her to step back and brace against the door. "You an' father won't let me leave the house anyway. And when I decided I wanted to me self." His father's words were like the dragons of Elsa's stories, their flames beating on his shield as did the sudden change against his mind. "I'll prove I can be around people. He says I can't look at people, well, I looked at you."

Alfred's mother leaned against the door, resting her head to her hand. The doors wooden finish pressed hard against the leather of the couch's armrest. Alfred took a step back, breathing heavily. He glanced at the clock, finding Gwen would be here in twenty-five minutes.

"Yes, and it is quite frightening." She swallowed while regaining her balance. "So, if I am to understand if there is to be any change, you wish it to be at a public school?"

"Yes."

Alfred's heavy breathing subsided, finding she understood. A question rose in his mind once his eyelids relaxed. Regret weighed on them like the stacks of books he piled up after finishing each one. How could he be so brave toward her but not toward his father who he feared the most?

"I'm sorry, Mum. I just have no friends beyond Gwen."

"And I am sorry as well, Alfred." she said, fainting a smile. "You have never been one for change. To see you wishing to make such a large one..." She moved closer and knelt to hug him, but he backed away. "That is another thing you must improve on." Her eyes sank with her chin as if a hug would raise them from their sadness.

Through the years, Alfred, for some reason, had resented her affection. He looked at her, remembering the little kisses on the cheek before bed. And how he would wipe the moist feeling left on his cheek with his sleeve. Was she right? Was this something else he needed to fix? He took a step toward her still open arms and allowed them to ease around him. A bit of comfort rushed through him, though his eyes had transfixed on the clock again.

Alfred pulled away when the doorbell chimed. *She early?* Josephine stepped back and gave him a slight smile, then went to let Gwen in. Alfred straightened his waist jacket as the friend he was soon to lose entered. They spoke of what had just transpired and of what a public school was like, its school bells, numerous halls, and rooms. There were names too. If he were to make friends, Alfred would have to learn those as well. He rubbed his fingers hoping the other boys enjoyed fairytales as much as him. *What if they like kickin' a ball around like 'em kids across the street?* By the end of their session, what he wished to do frightened him more than the challenges he'd read of Hercules.

When they were at the front door, Alfred hugged Gwen the way his mother hugged him, but only briefly. Her mole still bothered him, especially now in those four seconds. The door clicked shut after Josephine said her own goodbyes. It was then that he noticed something he hadn't before.

"Mum. You're gettin' fat."

Josephine spun, pressing her back hard against the door as a shock expanded across her lips and eyes.

"Alfred, that is something you most certainly cannot say to anyone." She moved to the looking glass left of the study's door. "I will say that until this moment you have proven yourself to your father."

The insecurity in her voice made him break the eye contact he was trying to master. Yet when he looked up at her again, her reflection spoke differently than her words. To him, though, she was still angry.

"Sorry, I'll try not to, Mum. You don't make fun of me height. So, I shouldn't make fun of you or—"

"Or others," she finished for him. "Dinner will be ready in a few hours. You have proven yourself."

There was a hint of pride in her words mixed with a touch of weariness Alfred could not understand. She was right though, and his father would know of his goodbye to Gwen. It had to convince Charles of his readiness. Until then, he let the face his mother had made in the looking glass go. Returning to the study, Alfred pushed himself up onto the couch after grabbing another book.

Dinner passed as quickly as the hours leading to it. Alfred told his father of the goodbye to Gwen, leaving out her mole. He added his mother's hug to the tale and left out the remark about her weight. She gave him a wink, flashing a smile once the story ended.

The fading blond of Charles beard loosened its usual tight grip when he said, "Well done." Then a grin emerged, usually reserved for guests at parties that Alfred tried to avoid, except this grin he did not like, making him break eye contact. "The arrangements will be made in the morning. And if you prove you can handle it, then we shall see how you do elsewhere."

Blocking out the rest of what was said, Alfred held onto the first compliment Charles had ever given him. Finishing his supper, he slid off the chair muttering quietly over and over *well done*.

Five days passed with no word from his father, making Alfred incredibly nervous. At the end of the day, he ascended the stairs, eyes closed. The wait was too much. He slammed his door, sending vibrations down the stairs and rattling the wall until the glass encasing an oil sconce fell, shattering on the steps. He paced back and forth across the rug and scratched at the back of his head. *What taking so long?*

Rain tapped like a woodpecker against the window. The tapping had been muffling the chiming clock tower for days, but he had not taken advantage of the restful sleep it offered him. As he readied for bed, thoughts raced faster than usual. They halted as the door creaked opened to reveal his father.

"You start school tomorrow." Charles said. Alfred's lips widened. Charles barely flinched, stiffening, and curling his own lips in disgust soon after. "It will be in more advanced classes than others." His father eased the door until it was almost shut while glaring at him. Alfred jumped up and down, twirling and giggling, only to stop when he realized his father was unamused. "You have your tutor to thank for that." A bitterness rang in his words "She says you're too smart for the other boys."

Alfred did his best to stand still. Nothing would spoil this moment. Not even the fact that he would be in tougher classes or how unimpressed his father was.

"Thank you," Alfred said, beginning the conversation again with a gratitude he never thought possible. "I can't wait to have friends. You don't know how—"

"There will be more to it than friends," Charles said. "If your studies slip in the slightest, I shall pull you out."

Alfred grinned, keeping his eyes focused and trying to block out the threat. Schoolwork would be the easy part. All that mattered was leaving the house and ending the loneliness.

"I'll keep them up, Father," he said. "You have me word."

Lightning clapped, flashing against the green of Charles's eyes and sending a shudder down Alfred's back. His father's eyes seemed to glow green for a brief moment then fade.

"That had best be done."

The door slammed shut, rattling the walls, leaving Alfred to continue his jumping and twirling, every spin raising his spirits. He hopped up into bed, flinging his slippers with the tips of his toes. They fell short of the bathroom door, making two clopping sounds. Pulling up the covers, the tiny legs of loneliness didn't creep up his back, nor did he find the need to read. His eyes shut as he tried to picture what his first day of school might be like. And then his mind began to question why his father had sounded so unhappy. Also, what strange glow was in his eyes. Alfred had seen it only once long ago. *He doesn't like me happy.*

Sleep absorbed his worries, shaping into a vast stretch of land. Ever-rising hills encompassed it, blanketed in trees of every kind that Alfred had read about. In the distance, within the valley of green, stood a brick building enclosed by a fence of black bars. Storm clouds brewed over it, darkening what he knew to be the school Anna had described. Lightning clapped, making him run just when tiny droplets tapped the grass. His legs ached the faster he ran. The grass was slick, chilling his toes as he found he wasn't wearing any shoes. Red-bricked columns held the fence together, all sprouting from two large ones supporting an arch. Children appeared through the bars going toward and then to the right and left of what was a small white tower above. Thunder roared, sounding like a lioness, sending heavier rain drops like saliva from her hungry jaws. In the storm's rage, Alfred missed a stone in plain sight.

"Ugh," he grunted, falling forward, his tongue tasting mud.

Lightning flashed across the sky, blinding him for seconds like the mud down his face, forcing him to squint at the school. Every child beyond the fences looked different now. Some were fully grown while others remained young. Some were disfigured. Others were as small as him, shadowed by those passing for giants. He wiped the mud from his eyes, but when the last of it was gone, the children were too. Searching amongst the school's barred fence, Alfred sank into the mud, finding himself alone, hoping he wouldn't be at school.

Seconds passed, and there was still no sign as to where the children could have gone to. The mud was about his waist now. The school's bricks darkened the more it rained, and Alfred either had to move or be swallowed. Reaching and churning through the mud, his hands found the puddle's edge but only after several long minutes. When he was free, the school was almost a blur in the heavy rainfall. Alfred took off at a sprint. Globs of mud added weight to his short legs. Finally, he reached the gate. He pushed at the bars with his muddy fingers, bars so cold they chilled him until he awoke within his room.

An hour passed until Alfred was fully dressed in his school uniform. Adjusting it, the sleeves were a little long on the crested coat, and the pant legs hid his shoes. He looked up at the clock. Time was running short, so he rolled his pant legs inward while doing his best to ignore the sleeves. Alfred moved out to the stairs and froze. The steps proved scarier than before with his oversized uniform.

"Come, Alfred. You mustn't be late." His mother poked her head out of the dining room. Her eyes lit up when she saw how he looked in the uniform. "You look just like your father." She looked back to the clock in the dining room. "If you hurry, you shall be punctual just like him as well."

A creak of her chair led the slow flopping his pant legs made as they unraveled. Sweat flung from his forehead, searching for a swift way down the stairs. Thinking quicker than he had ever done, Alfred mounted the railing. Bit by bit, he slid himself until the globe at the bottom pressed against his butt. Opening his eyes, he sighed, finding he had proven himself to be Elsa's little knight.

After breakfast came the carriage along with something he had only sampled through his home's windows wind—wind accompanied by the smells of the world. Some were unpleasant and others more so, but he welcomed it all as the carriage sped off with him and his mother in it.

The clop of horse hooves blended with the rustle of tree branches shading businesses and homes. Alfred peered through the tiny window at the back of the carriage. A light breeze cooled the back of his neck. The seat was low enough that he had to stand on it, his blonde hair just brushing the Richards crest gracing the windows top. Its overhanging canopy gave them shade, and when he saw a couple cross the street, it amazed him to see them from a place not his room for once. Josephine sat beside him with the circular straw hat meant to complete his uniform resting on her lap.

Alfred sat back down as the carriage hit a misshapen cobblestone. The smell of horse droppings made him weary for his first steps. Eventually, they passed under an arch similar to the one in his dream, yet this one had a gold lion at is center. Above was a coat of arms making it seem as though the lion was balancing it on his head.

"We're here, Alfred. Harrow School for Boys," Josephine said.

Alfred crouched a little from her adjusting the hat on his head. He took the brim in his hands before she could fit it properly.

"Good luck then." She pulled her fingers away. "I'm proud of you, my son."

"Thank you, Mum. I...I'll keep me grades up." He climbed down the tiny steps, maneuvering through on the carriage's U-shaped door, trying to keep balance. "Goodbye," he said without looking at her.

The school loomed like a mountain with trails leading to the right and left of its midpoint. A tiny white clock tower above told him his wishes would soon start. A horse snorted as the carriage and his mother left him to be lost in the crisscross of other similarly dressed boys. Alfred's heart pounded when they stopped to stare, but he kept walking. They didn't stop even after the stairs left him panting. Alfred tried to look at them, hearing whispers, fending them off with a smile.

Letting out a sigh as he closed the door, he pulled out the papers showing where his first class was. More stares followed the earlier ones, except these could all be seen. The sun did not hide them in the partly shaded hall. He quickened his pace until his classroom's number loomed overhead in black. In there, he kept silent until the room filled, and class began.

Chapter 3

Days passed with Alfred keeping to his studies. Constant stares from other boys turned to irritated looks every time he answered a question right, which happened every single time, leaving many and himself wishing the professor would call on another. This morning, Alfred stooped low in his seat until only his eyes could be seen. He tried to keep his hand down despite the other boys not knowing the answers he did.

After leaving class at noon, Alfred entered the lunchroom. It was large, and it echoed with voices that blurred together into one solid sound. So far, the wish to make friends had not come easy the way it had with Gwen and Elsa. When he made it to one of the crowded tables, he waved, shouting over the noise to introduce himself. Some of the boys were from his class. They whispered to the others, and then almost as if it had been rehearsed, they stood and left. Their retreat left the chairs disheveled and him alone among them. Alfred hopped up on one and ate until only one pea remained. He slid the green orb from side to side, waiting for the bell to ring.

"Why, hullo there."

The voice revealed a fat boy wearing the messiest uniform Alfred had ever seen. It was misbuttoned with many stains and wrinkles. Some of it seeped over his belt like a white curtain over the boy's flabby belly. The boy sat beside him, joined by another with a faintly growing beard and hair freshly parted to one side.

"They call me John Rosekuh the fourth, and yours?"

Alfred crinkled his nose, focusing on the pea. The stench from John's teeth was almost worse than the horse droppings lining his way to school this morning. Neither boy appeared friendly, nor did the third plopping himself in a chair across from him. This one was the shortest of the three. He grabbed Alfred's plate, sliding it swiftly to the end of the table until it crashed on the floor. Other boys looked up only to return to their lunches almost frightened.

"Answer my brother, or the plate won't be the only thing to go sliding." said the short boy.

From the left to the middle and the right, he glanced at each and said, "Alfred. Alfred Richards."

"Richards?" The fuzzy boy gaped. "Are you Charles the Butcher's whelp?"

"I'm not a puppy."

John squeezed his shoulder. Alfred made a face, trying to pull away, but John's sausage fingers clamped tighter.

"That's right," said John. "You're a whelp."

"No." Alfred tried to turn to correct John, but his shoulder ached. "That's what a whelp es...a puppy."

Slap, the short boy's hand went across Alfred's face. "You are not to correct my big brother."

"Technically you're the biggest, Roger." John chuckled. "Though you are—"

"Shut up!" Roger yelled.

Alfred shuddered, rubbing his cheek where he'd been slapped.

The lunchroom went quiet. Hundreds of eyes gazed at them, making Alfred long for the familiar surroundings of his room and his father's study. The wish for freedom and friends was beginning to sound like the biggest mistake ever. The closer Roger's face came, the more John's grip tightened. Alfred tried to wiggle free only to cry out when a tiny crack went off in his shoulder.

"You think you're so smart, don't you?" Roger pinched Alfred's cheeks until his little fingers pressed against teeth.

"Please...leave me 'lone. I just want to keep t' me studies." Tears ran down Alfred's cheeks, and his hands shook.

Whispers filled the room like a sea of serpents about to crash its waves. Alfred tried again to twist free. The three brothers just stared, making wisecracks about his height, much the same as from his first time to school.

"Leave him *alone*, Roger," a strange sounding voice called out.

The crowd's whispering hastened to almost a humming as a boy approached the table. Alfred gasped once the two grips released. The three brothers turned their heads sharply like hawks finding another prey.

"Oh, look, it's the kike." Roger laughed. "Come to save the Butcher's whelp."

"I thought your people don't like little pigs like Richards here." John chuckled.

The boy made his way to the table until the brothers' laughs were so loud Alfred had to cover his ears. Before he knew it, his rescuer had him out of the lunchroom and into the hall. His hair was dark, and the uniform he wore was wrinkled. Alfred looked up to see if they were alone after having buried his face in the confines of his uniform.

"I am Jacob."

The boy's accent was nothing Alfred had ever heard before, not even at his father's cocktail parties where the accents numbered in the dozens. He thought this might be his chance to make a friend. He noticed Jacob's nose was slightly bent, but unlike with his mother and her weight, Alfred kept his thoughts in his head this time.

"Alfred Richards," said Alfred. "Thank you for saving me. I thought they were goin' t' hurt me."

They continued down the hall at an easy pace. Both realized before the lunchroom emptied behind them that they shared the last two classes. Alfred's nerves and the pain in his shoulder settled the more they talked. Jacob was from Poland, just miles from the capital, and had lived in London for three years.

When they were at the door to history class, Alfred asked, "Why Roger call you that?"

Jacob's eyes lowered for a few seconds before returning to Alfred's face. Alfred wasn't sure why Jacob's shoulders had slumped when he asked.

"I am Jewish and, vell, if you have read the first few books of my people, you—"

Alfred reached up, placing a hand on Jacob's breast pocket. The curiosity whirled into what it should have been concern.

"You come from brave people. Exodus es me favorite of them all." Alfred guided his friend to an extra seat next to his at the back of the classroom. "I wish I could be brave like that," he said. "I'm glad you were, an' think we can be good friends."

They sat down as Jacob's frown quickly formed a smile. "Thank you. I think we will be too."

Other students entered, sliding chairs out quickly, pulling them the same, making squeaking sounds. A rattle of the room's door signaled that class was about to start. Alfred and Jacob focused on class until the clock aligned with the time they anxiously awaited. Though when the last class ended and they were at the school's main gate, a familiar sight told him time was short. In the distance, the box carriage he had arrived in was trotting toward them at a steady pace.

"We will have to talk more 'tween classes tomorrow," he said. "Mum is almost here."

Jacob's face looked weary while they watched boys leaving by foot and others by carriages pulled by well-groomed mares. From the look on his face, Alfred thought his friend might still be sad from lunch. Yet when he spoke, it was most welcoming.

"I can hardly wait. And if the Rosekuhs should bother you, ve'll face them together."

The carriage door swung open revealing a sour look on his father's face. His fingertips drummed impatiently over a solid gold cane head shaped like a meat tenderizer. A little smile crossed Alfred's face before the door was pulled shut. Charles tapped at the cabin's canvas while Alfred waved to Jacob. Jacob waved back until they were divided by the school's fence. Rain fell quickly on the carriage's roof like shoe soles within the school's halls. The carriage was dim with what little light came through the window, yet his father's face had a bit of light to it as they rounded a corner.

"I'm told you are at the top of the class," Charles said. "I suppose I'm to be proud of you."

Alfred's eyes met Charles's gaze. His heart almost seemed to remain steady despite how bitter his father appeared. *That's what father is—bitter*, Alfred thought, remembering asking Gwen what the word meant one day.

"Yes, I suppose... I'm doing well, which es what you wanted. I made a friend too."

Charles let out a snort. "Well, one part of the bargain has been kept. Now it's time my son learn the family trade."

Alfred gasped and his eyes widened.

"I never agreed to that."

"You most certainly did," Charles said. "I spoke of other things, one of which being the trade of a butcher."

The carriage slowed just as the rain did. Alfred didn't remember Charles ever mentioning it. All he could remember was being complimented and then days later told to keep his grades up or be pulled out. His heart flung itself against his chest when the driver opened the door.

"I've got school." Alfred cried. "I can't."

The carriage dipped when Charles avoided a small puddle below the parking step. "Get out," he snapped. "I'll not deprive you of schooling. A Richards honors his bargains."

Rain ran down his face just before his nose breathed in the scent of blood in the air. He gulped only to choke on it thanks to the narrow climb down. Any good feelings from school were now soggy like his hair.

"I am a Richards," said Alfred, chewing his lip, "and I will honor the deal."

His voice sounded apprehensive when he said it, but his father ignored it. They entered through red doors, one reading Prime and the other Meats in tall white letters. Pinching his nose, Alfred's eyes puckered the tighter he squeezed. He let it go before his father cocked his head back, pinching it shut again later. With each turn, his gaze stayed to the ground, following the taps of his father's cane against worn wooden planks.

The hard thud of meat cleavers almost in unison made him look up to see mounds of meat. Juices ran over cutting boards redder than the door he'd come through. Buckets caught shavings of fat and broken bone meshed and was speckled in red droplets. Alfred forced a swallow to fend off a surge of vomit, but it only made him dizzy. The men through the windows of each room they passed looked to be drowning in seas of blood. Closing his eyes for a second, he wondered if the slamming and hanging cow carcasses were what made his father so miserable. The carcasses were stripped bare of fur, somewhat steaming as if each animal had died only seconds ago.

When they were at the building's rear, Charles hung his hat before sitting behind a large, cluttered desk. Clunky footsteps announced a man his father had called from the hall and now entered the office.

"Alfred will be joining you for this evening's duties," Charles said without looking up.

The man nodded, motioning to Alfred with two fingers gloved in black and doused with blood droplets. Alfred looked up at his father, seeing him scribble something out with a worn-down pencil.

"Father," he groaned, only to be directed by the pencil's dull point to the man halfway out the door.

His head sank into his chest as he followed the man until they were within a window-enclosed room. It was cleaner than the others with rolls of white paper stacked on one end of a table. A cart piled high with meat cutlets of different sizes sat on the other. The man tossed him a pair of gloves, which Alfred dropped. The table was too high to wrap the meat as the man was showing. Pulling up a stool from near the door, Alfred thought it was either try or likely never see Jacob again. Though his father had said it differently, the smell made him paranoid. To make matters worse, his father always worked late, and the gloves were baggy.

Grabbing the stool's top, he climbed it as it rattled beneath him. Every new cut he wrapped made fighting the encroaching vomit even harder. The gloves made it even worse, sliding up and down his hands. Across the table, the man wrapped his portions faster than Alfred could fold a corner. Everyone revealed lines of red meant to stay concealed. After a third attempt on a fifth cut, Alfred tossed it at one of the windows. It plopped against the glass, then slowly slid to the ground.

By now his hands were slippery and the gloves were filled with sweat, forcing him to yank them off. His hands shook and slipped when he tried to tear a sheet from the paper roll. The man continued, making no move to help, and showing no sign of concern. Alfred tried one last time, fingers shaking, crinkling the paper.

"I can't do this!"

Then it came with a rush so fast the peas of lunch looked like seashells washing up on a red and brown shore. Milk formed the bubbly, foaming tide making the black-gloved man stumble away. Alfred hopped off the stool when the man fell alongside it to the floor. Running back the way he'd come, Alfred turned in time to see his father rise from the desk.

The way out was close, and his legs were aching like his head. Footsteps followed until a hand pressed against the door when he grabbed the knob. Alfred's hand dropped, clasping around his mouth to shield his puckering, wet lips.

"Work has not finished." Charles's hand balled into a fist, pressing hard against the door. "You have made a mess. *Go!* Clean it up."

Alfred panicked, trying the knob again.

"Do it!" Charles punched the door. "You will honor your word."

"How can I if I don't remember agreeing to it?" Alfred screamed. "I can't. I'm no butche."

Alfred looked around, finding he had been backed into a corner. The vomit rose again even faster now that his father had him trapped. Swallowing it in one gulp, his eyes watered.

"Fine! If my own son shall not honor his bargains and embarrass me at my own establishment"—Charles yanked opened the door. Wind and heavy rain turned the floor's wood black— "then tomorrow will be your last day of school. Get out!"

A horse snorted as Charles pointed to their carriage to the left of the shop's entrance. His father opened the door while instructing the driver to return at the usual time. Alfred climbed in to hear the door slam and a puddle splash when his father returned to work. Easing forward, the carriage pulled away as Alfred wrung out the rainwater from his tie. His hands shook—not from how cold or wet he was but from knowing tomorrow would be his last day at school. His last day having a friend. And almost worse, his freedom would follow it. Again, bravery had escaped him just as it had with the Rosekuhs.

It had never truly returned since losing Elsa. He pushed back his hair, resting himself on the black leather of the carriage's seat. The dampness of his uniform made the cool leather seat send a shiver up and down his back.

The briefly dormant loneliness that once crept up his back ascended again once the faint squeak of the carriage wheels ceased. Easing down to the ground, the front door swung open. His mother loomed over him as he climbed the last step. Her current disposition made him realize she knew already what had happened. He flinched when she slammed the door shut, sending droplets everywhere. The stairs to his room seemed higher this time. Quickly, Alfred's eyes shut, blocking out the lingering disappointment on his mother's face.

At the middle of the next day, Alfred sat down to lunch, finding that his appetite had disappeared once Jacob plopped down next to him. There wasn't any need for him to say a word. Alfred had not changed his uniform since yesterday and his hair was a mess of tangles. Jacob said nothing, both letting the voices of other boys do the talking for a while. Alfred swallowed a bit of spaghetti, twirling another mouthful before a hand rested on his shoulder. Looking up, he found Jacob smiling. He quickly pulled away, pushing his plate aside, and then buried his face in his hands.

"What's wrong, Alfred? You are not your clean-pressed self."

Alfred kept his hands wrapped tight, sniffing back tears only for them to run rampant.

"We can't be friends no more…"

"Why?" Jacob said, gaping. 'We met only yesterday."

Peeking over his fingers, he hoped Jacob didn't think it was anything he had done. Yet how could he tell him that he made a bargain including terms he didn't remember. That he would have had to work at his father's business to be allowed to go to school. And that because of sheer frustration, and a weak stomach, the two would have to part ways.

"Father wanted me to work for him, and I made a mess of it." *Sniff.* "I...embarrassed him."

"So, is he pulling you out of school?"

Alfred nodded, pulling his plate toward him. He stirred the interwoven noodles, forming a ball on his fork.

"I'm sorry." he sniffed. "It's all me fault."

Silence made a wedge between them for a while longer. Alfred turned to his friend for a moment, wanting to say more. He stuff himself with a mouthful of noodles when he couldn't find the words. The silence ended once trouble came strolling toward them in threes. The Rosekuhs hovered around their table like buzzards over a carcass.

"Well, if it isn't Christ's killer," Roger said, removing his sneer on Jacob and focusing it on Alfred, "and his demon friend."

Mind swirling, Alfred pictured Jacob nailing Jesus to the cross. Jacob gave Roger a look as John and the fuzzy brother laughed. Then Alfred realized it was a joke but not a funny one.

"I hear you're leaving us, Richards," John snorted. "Heard you spilled your guts all over some tasty meats."

Alfred looked up at the fat boy, flabbergasted.

"Our father saw the whole thing," the fuzzy brother said. His peach fuzz had grown out since yesterday to a more noticeable set of patches. "He made out good, though. Your father paid him extra for cleaning up the mess."

Alfred remembered the man stumbling away from the milk dripping onto the floor. The meat cutlets had been drenched and the ones wrapped were soggy. The Rosekuhs circled him and Jacob like hungry sharks.

"I am sorry for making him clean me mess," said Alfred.

John's fingers clasped down on Alfred's shoulder, but Alfred slid from the chair before they could tighten. The three brothers backed away just as the chair banged. His hands formed fists when Jacob tried to halt the coming storm.

"He said he vas sorry. Now go."

"Shut up, big nose!" Roger yelled. "The midget wants to fight."

Looking down at his hands and then up at the brothers, Alfred stood still. There wasn't much to lose, and by the day's end, he would be alone again. His fists flew into the groin of the fuzzy brother, making the boy fall and cough. When Alfred turned to John, his right fist was swallowed by John's turning stomach. John grunted as he went to pull his brother off the ground, then he backhanded Alfred. Alfred collapsed, blood and tears running into his curled lips. Jacob knelt down to help him only to be struck across the cheek by Roger.

The other students formed a circle around them. Alfred struggled to his feet, helping Jacob as best he could.

"Are you okay, Jacob?"

Jacob rubbed his cheek, then touched Alfred's shoulder. "Your braver den you think."

The two stood as the three brothers joined, pressing them against the table brandishing readied fists. The room roared with cheers for the two friends. Both were about to make a stand when professors entered, shouting for all to return to lunch. They did, but Alfred, Jacob, and the brothers weren't so lucky. The professors soon had them all separated. Two professors lifted Alfred from the ground. Jacob and he were rushed through the lunchroom doors to the hall. Curses rang out from the Rosekuhs calling Alfred a coward and Jacob a filthy rat. Peering back at the shutting doors, Alfred caught a glimpse of Roger punching a professor.

Soon, Alfred was plopped in a desk beside Jacob as a scolding ensued unlike any Alfred had ever had. Panting, he closed his eyes and clasped his ears. Then the bell rang.

Chapter 4

Evening came fast the way it always did. The last day of Alfred's greatest wish was over, and in a few short minutes, dinner would commence. Only the streetlamps flickering through the bowed window in the dining room gave any light. It shifted from side to side on the hardwood of the second step. He stared at the light, ignoring the soft click of the maid's heels followed the heavy flap of the swaying kitchen door. The chandelier hissed when the maid lit a long, thin match to give color to the gas. The little flames broke up the darkness once each was lit, yet their dances made him feel worse, knowing he would be seeing more of them.

Minutes passed with the table being set, then his mother entered from the kitchen. She sat down without bothering to summon him as she usually did. Instead, the smell of steak, boiled potatoes, and peas did. Seeing the peas, he gagged aloud as he entered. Josephine paid him no mind when his tongue tasted bile, reminding him of the slaughterhouse. Climbing the chair, he held the churning within his stomach back, covering his mouth from a dry heave. As he rubbed his eyes, his mother still paid him no notice. She stroked her stomach for what may have been the hundredth time and for some reason he could not discern. It didn't matter anyway. Not much did now that he was alone again. He held on to one small comfort, though.

Looking down, he ran his fingers over the figure upon the book he'd been reading.

The story was an old one, reminding Alfred of his first friend and of Jacob who would appear to be his last. The book was worn, and the pages fox eared, but the knight remained unmoved by the danger around him. The wish to read it again was to be reminded of Gwen as well. Its chief character was brave, tall, and free to travel the world unimpeded. Alfred wished he could do the same and go as far away from home as possible.

Keeping his eyes focused on his meal, the study door clicked shut. He thought his father was leaving to join the two men he'd heard from upstairs earlier, but heavy footfalls from behind signaled a first as his father joined them. Alfred didn't look up, fearing if he did that a scorning may commence. Instead, forks pierced cooked meat and knives sawed slivers. All three kept to their business just inches away for several minutes. Metal severed the silence and the petals of a china-plate, breaking the trance Alfred was in.

"Nothing?" Charles held his utensils erect as if they were sentries with spears at the ready. "Not one word of complaint." Metal thudded hard against the tablecloth. "Not even a mumbled apology."

Josephine placed a small square of steak in her mouth, chewed, and then swallowed.

"Alfred," she whispered, "your father is addressing you. Answer!"

Not wanting to look up, Alfred wondered if an apology would do any good. His father's heavy breathing made its way across the table.

"I'm sorry, Father," Alfred said. His father's heavy breathing sucked in like a dragon preparing to breathe flame. "I did not honor our bargain."

Charles exhaled, pulling his napkin from his collar, and then slamming it on the table.

"Minutes of production were lost. If I had known my own son was so weak of stomach, I'd have never wasted my time enrolling you in that school." Alfred's grip tightened around his book, bracing for another blast of what he wished would soon end. "And to further embarrass the Richards name, you started a fight in—"

"They were teasing me and Jacob. I stood up for us."

"And you did so in a most impolite fashion," said Charles. "Now any future Richards cannot attend the school."

Alfred looked at his parents, finding himself confused. Josephine sipped her water, looking toward Charles and giving him a nod. A slight grin spread across Charles's face, making Alfred grip the book tighter.

"As smart as that tutor of yours claims you are," his father said, planting his hands upon the table. "Being observant does not precede it."

His book slid forward, forcing his fingertips to lunge for the author's name and finding it before the book fell. His mouth gaped for seconds, finding an answer to the mirror mystery days earlier.

"Mum, you're... You're pregnant."

Josephine nodded, feeling her stomach again.

Charles weaved his fingers together, still grinning as the study door opened. Alfred's palms were sweaty, and his mind froze. The floor creaked. Still not breaking his gaze, Alfred thought the sound was the maid. Not even the deep labored cough not belonging to her did it. Not until a shadow had darkened the white tablecloth did he turn and find...

"What is—" Alfred yelped. The two men grabbed his shoulders, lifting him fast and hard.

Thud went the book of his childhood, growing distant with the floor. "Father, Mum, what's go in on?"

He twisted and turned, kicking at air. Charles rose, moving to Josephine's side, still grinning. Josephine's face aged as Alfred's eyes blurred with tears. He thought she was sad too, but she would not move to save him. Alfred cried for her, watching her chin sink into her chest. Charles gently gripped her shoulders as the front doorknob twisted.

"Another shall take your place, Alfred." Charles said. "This one shall not be a dwarf and will learn to honor the family name."

"Please." Alfred looked at the book. The wish to be brave rose with the sound of rain. "I will do better. See, Mother, I speak properly...I...Mum, pleeeease. Don't let 'em take me."

He gave one more twist, striking his head on something hard and pointed. Alfred shook his left arm free. The other man went into a coughing fit, freeing his other arm. He landed on his feet and then sank to his knees.

"Why, Father?" he yelled, rising, eyes focused on Charles. "I have always been little. You never trusted me with anything 'til recent."

Charles motioned for the two men to get on with it. They gripped Alfred's arms again. One man's hand was sticky from the cut Alfred had given him.

"The Richards family has always produced a perfect stock of men and women without a flaw to be seen. Your mother convinced me to trust in you after all this time." Charles let go of Josephine's shoulders as the two men carried Alfred back toward the door. "I told her there must be another child should you fail. This was long in the making, and as I told her many months ago, 'He will fail as big as he is little.'"

"Then why allow me t' live here so long? Why not sooner?"

The rain grew louder when the coughing man opened the door. Droplets tapped Alfred's back as his mother looked up to give a final answer.

"We tried many times after your birth, Alfred, to have another. I may have found your speech grotesque, but I have always loved you. Charles, he—"

"That will be enough, Josephine," Charles said. His father pointed when she tried to rise. "Take him now."

Alfred pressed a foot against the doorway as the men tried to pull him and the door shut.

"You what, Father?" Groaning, he struggled, his foot slipping on the wet doorway.

Charles clasped the rim of his wine glass with his rough fingers, sipped, and then scowled.

"I cannot and will not stand to have the Richards legacy broken because I sired an abomination. The next shall erase you from it and make things as they should be."

After one final tug from the two men, Alfred's foot gave way. The door slammed shut in the split second he saw his mother move forward, only to be forced to sit by his father. Outside, the rain made murky his father's return to the table's head. The rain fell faster, drowning his screams, turning the street into a cobbled river of browns. Through the bow window's murky panes, his mother begged until his father raised an open palm and slapped her cheek. Alfred turned his head when he heard the sound of metal scratching metal.

A black carriage with a small square window opened its door. To either side were two small lamps struggling within the storm. Alfred twisted faster and kicked harder, splashing water all over each man's pants. The one with the bloodied chin gripped the tightest, making Alfred's arm go numb. It only loosened slightly as they climbed up into the carriage. Another man shut the door, leaving only the square window for light.

Clenching his teeth, the men yanked his arms back. *Snap! Snap!* Alfred moved toward the window, only to be tugged back by his restraints. Quickly the carriage wheels sloshed through the flooded streets. Fishtailing around a corner, the carriage sent Alfred into one man's lap. He grunted, pushing Alfred to his feet again. As they made their way, streetlamps flashed through the tiny window.

Easing himself to the floor, his legs strained without arms to balance. A sudden stop helped him down, bruising his tailbone. He tried to wipe his tears with a shoulder only to have a chill sent down his spine. Time and again, he wanted to ask where his father was sending him. The two men whispered amongst themselves. One was still cursing Alfred for the blow to the chin. Nothing but their white coats could be seen in the quick flashes of light. After the carriage struck a fifth broken cobblestone, he decided not to ask.

"Sure, I'm not perfect," he whispered as the flashes gave brief glimpses of his arms and legs. "And I not da best spoken—"

"Shut your yap and save it for the doctor." The coughing man launched a wad of mucus just as the door opened.

"What doctor?" The other man chuckled. "He's joining the other nuts in the can. And in the can, you be talking to your own nuts."

Two more men grabbed Alfred's arms as the first two removed his restraints. Rain tapped against an awning of worn wood above. Everything was dimly lit until twin doors creaked open to reveal a hall lined top to bottom with white tiles. They were brightened by oil lamp sconces, revealing doors and passages. Alfred looked down at the floor as a rat scurried by. Shutting his eyes and shaking his head, the rat was gone, but the smell of mildew replaced it. They passed over a puddle at the same time a tap on his head revealed where its source came from.

"What is this place?" he cried. The cold droplet ran down his forehead, making him shiver. For a moment there was no answer except for the screams up and down the halls. "Please tell me."

"Does it matter?" The man holding his left arm grunted. "No one leaves once they're in here."

"That can't be true." Alfred sniffed. "You work here. You get to leave, don't you?"

The two men laughed as a third unhooked a ring of keys from his belt. They clicked together when the right one was found.

"Just the monsters. We keep them locked up and fed." The key turned as the third man pulled open the door. "Here's your cage, monster."

The men maneuvered him sideways through the door as Alfred took in his new home. Every wall was covered in numbers. Each one looked to be etched by something jagged and sharp. Some he had seen in the older books within his father's study. They looked to be just as useless and boring. A few calculations encircled delicately painted angels. The shadows made them look disfigured. Most he'd seen when passing churches on the way to school. Alfred gasped when the two men dropped him on the bed. They were still laughing seconds before the door slammed shut and the bed springs had stop creaking.

Aside from a small window above the bed, there wasn't much light. Alfred settled into the bed, pressing the lumps flat with his palms only for them to rise again. A toilet with no flusher stood across the room to the right of the door. It was haloed too by more numbers, but these were left to right instead of up to down. He eased down to gather his thoughts, finding the bed smelled of piss.

Father may have wanted me gone, he thought looking up at a young woman cradling her child, the colors more vibrant than any the angels possessed, *but Mum may still come.* As the pillow formed around his head, Alfred's nerves settled a little as he looked up at the figures. *Mum does love me. And she said so.* This one stood alone from the others. Her beauty matched his mother's and the way she looked at the child gave him hope. *Maybe Mum will come.*

His eyes grew heavy, shutting as the moonlight shifted toward the other images. The piss smell lingered in his nose even as he pulled his shirt over it. The top button snapped off when his nose pressed behind it.

A key turning and a quick tug of the door broke what felt like only seconds since he had shut his eyes. Like most mornings after a nightmare, scolding, or argument, Alfred was calm again, though he wished he was looking at his room instead of what passed for a dirty loo. The dreary morning light bathed the faces of his captors from last night. Alfred pressed himself against the wall only to be heaved to his feet. One man pressed a bar of soap atop fresh clothes and a towel against his chest.

"Here, wash up."

Alfred looked for a tub but could not see one.

"There's no place to."

The two men parted, gesturing toward a sink exactly right of the toilet. Alfred waddled toward it, undressing until the coughing man snorted back what had to have been a huge glob of mucus.

"Can you two leave, please?" Alfred peered over his shoulder. "I'm gettin' started."

One man turned the left knob. The faucet rattled until water spat out in quick bursts. "We're supposed to make sure you can."

Alfred gave them both a queer look. "But I can."

The two men crossed their arms, muttering to each other. Alfred unfastened the last button of his shirt, ready to remove it, but hoped the men would leave first.

"Good," one guard said, motioning the other to the door. "Cause none of the others can, especially the fat bitch."

The door slammed before the water finally turned hot. Yanking his hand back, the water stung his skin like hot needles. He tried to cool the water with the other knob, only to find there wasn't one. Burning minutes passed, leaving every inch of skin red. He patted the towel up and down and all over, rushing to end the use of its itchy fabric. All the while he ran down a list in head as to what breed of bitch she was and why she was sent to an asylum instead of a kennel.

Before even getting fully dressed in the gray button-down shirt and pants, the door swung open again. A plate slid to a stop once the door slammed shut. A growl from his stomach made his curiosity leave. He had not eaten since last night. Grabbing what looked to be a sliver of carrot from the pile of mush, he bit it. It tasted better than the whole dished looked, so he dug in.

Finishing, Alfred banged on the door, wondering again the kind of dog the guards had spoken of. When the door opened, a hand took the plate, then the door slammed shut faster than he could speak. Alfred banged on the door again. His nerves tightened when a metallic whoosh ran overhead.

"What you banging about?"

Seeing only the window's lip, Alfred took a few steps back. "Will I get to leave me room an' play with the fat dog?"

The man stared at him for a moment. Some of the window's light revealed red stubble growing from his chin over a small cut.

"There is no dog. It's a girl, you lug. Now quit all that banging. Or you'll tasting the back of my hand before the day is through."

Another swoosh halted any chance for further questions. Alfred returned to the bed, overwhelmed by another nose full of the piss smell. A slight smile made its way across his lips. Though he was disappointed to again not meet a dog in person, his father had not completely locked him away from the world. The loneliness that used to crawl up his back didn't return, knowing another chance to make a friend was ahead.

Tomorrow came with new clothes and a fresh towel. This time, he found the water was cooler at the beginning. He turned the knob on and off in spurts to avoid the stinging of yesterday. When the door opened to take his plate, two men ushered him down the hall. Doors along the way hung wide open, revealing torn-open beds, brown-stained walls, and cracked windows. Alfred kept his eyes to the floor, trying not to imagine how so much shit could cover so many walls.

Two wide doors swung open to his left, releasing noise that hurt his ears from those older and younger than him. Three guards tried to settle down a man beating on another in a corner. Three girls spun in circles until two of them fell. And when they did, the one still standing cheered and danced. The room was like the circuses he'd read about in the newspapers. Except this one, with its variety of tables and chairs, had no lions or elephants climbing them. Many were broken with teeth marks up and down their legs. Several, though, seemed to act like a cage around someone in the corner, far from all the others. Alfred's nose wrinkled when he realized who it was and that the guards had told the truth.

Alfred tried to approach her, avoiding the wish to pinch his nose as the doors closed. Two guards moved in front of them, bracing for the continuing fight. With each step, there was an obstacle, from the twirling girls to the fight spreading to the room's center. He gulped, almost choking on the smell. He tugged his right foot away before a loose hand from the fight could grab it.

"Hullo." He climbed a chair, gasping as he tried to introduce himself. "I'm Alfred Richards." He couldn't take it. Alfred pinched his nose. "Sorry, it just—"

"It's fine. I know I stink, and no need to look at me." She rubbed her stomach, which slid out in rolls from under her shirt, and then she smiled at Alfred. "I'm Maggie, Maggie O'Shea. Richards, you say? I love your steaks. Or...I did."

"My father's, not mine." Alfred's voice sounded rubbery the harder he pinched his nose. "He sent me here cause I'm a dwarf. I think also 'cause...oh, never mind."

The two sat silent for a bit, exchanging brief looks. Alfred found himself wishing to ask how she had become so fat. And then he remembered what his mother had said while looking at his legs and hands. But when his fingers loosened and dropped, he couldn't help himself.

"So how you get so fat?" Alfred immediately clasped a hand across his mouth.

"It's okay." She sniffed, rubbing away emerging tears. "At least ye were brave enough to come and sit by me."

Alfred looked at her for a moment, lowering his hand though not feeling brave but mean. Listening to Maggie explain, he now understood how cruel his father had truly been. Maggie's father had lost everything when the economy crashed for a time years ago. By then she had already been rather large. When her mother died, she'd eaten more, and with needing to sell the horses, her father couldn't provide for her. Tears ran down her red cheeks as she told Alfred the end.

"I've been here since I was thirteen. Da put me here 'cause it's run by the city." Her whole body shook as she covered her mouth, making Alfred wish to comfort her. "What those twirlin' girls don't eat, I do. I can't stop. You must think I'm..."

Alfred rose, moving aside the chairs, and hugged her.

"I think nothing but that you need what I have craved most." He looked at her. She looked down and slowly hugged him. "A friend."

Chapter 5

A new routine formed with each day's passing; one Alfred wished included not only the lifeless buildings staring back at him through the window but also his mother. Not a visit or letter came, yet he found comfort in Maggie's presence once the common room doors slammed shut. The pungent odor cascading from her unwashed body became what Alfred was growing to know. That and the horses she'd ridden and the races her father had won. She giggled when he mispronounced every breed he knew, making him frown for a moment.

"They make them more interestin' that way," she said, turning his shame to a giggle.

No books could be read to pass the time in his cell, so Alfred laid back on his pillow and tried to recall Elsa's stories. His eyes traced the sharply etched numbers encircling the morning-lit images. The curved and rough finishes of each number helped Alfred imagine that a wizard had carved them, one old and wise, residing in the village imprisoned within a mountain valley. Every story Elsa had told him began within one. The wizard always wore a hood, whispering counsel to the chosen champion. The words aiding in the champion's attempts at unhorsing another during the tournaments held at the base of the mountain.

The door creaked open as he pictured the villagers descending the mountain. Every one of them eagerly pushing and shoving, filling the arena's wooden stands. Brightly colored canopies shaded them while they aligned below banners sporting fierce beasts.

"Hullo, Alfred."

Alfred's eyes popped open as he turned to the door. His mind couldn't believe it, yet his eyes saw so clearly even in the dimness.

"Jacob." Alfred rose, moving a few steps, gulping, rubbing his eyes. They were clear like before, but again the assurance was needed. "How you find me?"

"Your mother told me vat happened." Jacob nodded at the guard, who closed the door. "She...," he said. "I had to know, so I found out the place you lived. I..."

Alfred embraced him, taking a step back. He gazed through tears at Jacob.

"She didn't want me t' go. I could tell that night. Thank you for coming." His thoughts turned to Maggie, sniffing back his delight when the friend he thought lost smiled. "I want you to meet somebody. She is really nice and is from Ireland."

"That is nice. I'm glad, but the man outside said we must stay in here."

Alfred's face wanted to collapse like bricks, but Jacob tried to add mortar to it to make him happy again.

"At least we get to see each other. It has been weeks since you stood up to the Rosekuhs."

"I been here weeks?" Alfred gasped. "It's felt like days." He moved to the bed, sinking into the mattress while letting the time spent locked up sink in.

Jacob sat beside him. The bedsprings whined at the added weight.

"We must get you out of here. Your mother told me how you tried to stand up to your father. Try again, and maybe he'll take you back."

Flashes of that night came and went in Alfred's mind, their brightness joined by the clap of thunder through the window above them. The same grin forming on his father's face, with the smell of peas replacing the bed's odor of piss. Alfred thrust himself up, moving to the sink, sweat pouring down his cheeks like the rain had done that night.

"No, he is our house's head. I broke the bargain." *Yet I can't remember agreeing to it.* "Remember?"

Alfred peered back to see Jacob rising, forming a grin, one that Alfred didn't understand.

"You have to stay positive, Alfred. True, a bargain has been broken, but I think you can convince him to take you back."

Kneeling, Jacob rested his hands on Alfred's shoulders. Their warmth gave Alfred a comfort long missed. The two were at eye level, which was something only Elsa had ever done when he was sad.

"I can't, Jacob. I'm a...abomination." His chin sank into his chest until his worries were worn and ugly like his shoes. "Always have, always will."

"Stop that." Jacob shook his shoulders. "Do you know how smart and kind you are?" Tears trickled down Jacob's face until the shaking eased to a stop. "Back home an' even here, my people are hated and spat on. When I saw you in the lunchroom alone, I thought..."

"Thought what?" Alfred's lips trembled at what he believed may have been the truth. "That I would... That you was not the only monster in class?"

Knocking away Jacob's hands, Alfred took a step back, fingers curled. He remembered how long the twelve years had been within his own home. *There was sound reasoning behind it.* Now his father's words made sense.

"At least you were free to come an' go." Alfred snapped. "If me father somehow does take me back. He'll just lock me up again in me room."

Jacob shook his head, rose, and moved slowly to the door before raising a hand.

"I sat with you," Jacob knocked on the door's worn surface,"so that I for once could have a friend. *Do widzenia,* Alfred."

The door slammed before the bed's creaking silenced from the heavy thud of Alfred's body. He pressed his face against the pillow. He had misjudged, overthought, and frightened away what was never gone. Now it was gone, and though he still had Maggie, the loneliness had made its grand return.

Alfred became distant with the passing of what felt like the second worst day of his life. The wish to have his clothes neat and his face washed for Maggie didn't seem to matter. Soap and towels piled up just as less food left his plate. His mother had tried to help him when he needed it most too. But for whatever reason, Alfred had allowed himself to do the same with Jacob. *Why do I assume the worst and say bad stuff?*

The next day, he didn't brace himself for the slam of the common room's doors. Their noise didn't faze him as much as the sight of what would become familiar surroundings. Looking out the window, Alfred pictured the look on Jacob's face in a windowpane. Slowly, he slumped into the corner away from the windows' light. The shadows dulled the asylum's gray uniform, whose sleeves slid to his elbows when he buried his face in his hands.

Each day to follow, he cuddled up in the same spot like a snail in its shell, his face buried in his hands. The soft footsteps of the twirling girls reminded Alfred of the rat he had seen his first night within the asylum. All three passed him, twirling in identical patterns every time he looked up. Sometimes one fell beside him, lying limp like a fish and smiling lifelessly like one until he shooed her away. They would giggle at him, returning every so often. Alfred wished the girls would ignore him like the others.

At noon the next day, a thud, louder and much, much heavier than the twirling girls could make, knocked Alfred over. He turned, edging a chair away from his head. It clanked against the table as he noticed something was different about his remaining friend. Her face was thinner, and the smell was gone, though she was still quite large.

"So, what's been bothering you?" Maggie said, her eyes a bit joyful as if she had some good news to share, though her tone was soft with sympathy. "Haven't seen ye in months."

Alfred shook his head. He found himself again amazed by the time vacuum surrounding the asylum. He forced himself to smile for her, though what bothered him made it hard to be happy.

"I made another mistake." He sniffed back its memory, resisting the urge to break down in tears. "Someone I knew came to visit." A heavy lump formed in his throat before he could finish.

Maggie wrapped a pillowy arm around his shoulder when he struggled to swallow. "From all the shouting ye did, sounds like a big one."

"How could you hear me? Your room is not near mine."

Maggie giggled.

"The guards talk a lot. They like prying into our business." She paused for a second when the twirling girls made their lap. "He is right. Ye need to stand up to your father. He can't be as tough as the meat he cuts."

Alfred grinned at that last bit. She, like Jacob, was right, but his father was the toughest man he knew.

"I want to, I really do, but I know me father, and he never changes nothing."

"If ye want something Alfred, ye have to try or else..." She breathed in, almost as if there was something she still wished to say beyond encouragement. "Or else why want it at all."

The wide common room's doors swung open revealing a man in a well-pressed brown sack coat with a buttoned-up, darker brown waistcoat. Maggie grabbed hold of a chair, pushing herself up as the man joined her once she stopped panting. Alfred put the pieces together.

"You're leavin'." He stood. The tiny legs crawled up his bottom until at the base of his spine. "Is this your father, the one who won all 'em races?"

The man nodded as Maggie welled up in tears.

"After I heard what happened between your friend and you, Da came and visited." She rubbed her eyes, wheezing through her words as she went on about how her father had found a job somewhere south of London, working with horses while allowing her to ride when she wanted.

Alfred almost wanted to ruin the excitement of the news, but there was regret mixed in her sobs.

"I wanted to be clean, and if I could, be thinner when this day came. I'm sorry I have to leave."

A peck on her cheek from her father made Alfred long for what they were soon to have again. *I want to be happy for 'em, but she is leavin' me.* He tried to form a smile that was sincere but couldn't.

"Please, take me with you," he said. "I have read about horses and how to groom fur."

"I'm sorry. Mr. Richards, is it?" Maggie's father said. "Meaning no offense, from what my daughter says, you're a smart lad. But we can't take ye cuz—"

"'Cause I'm a dwarf, isn't it?" Alfred snapped back. The same frustration surged in his stomach as it had with Jacob. Both Maggie and her father took a step back. "Maggie, I agreed with what you said before, but I is better off with you."

All three twirling girls made another pass by, and a boy began tapping his finger on the window when one of them spoke again.

"It's nothing to do with your height, lad. Legally, I can't, being you're not my son an' all."

"We can try to help convince your father to take you back, though," Maggie added.

Moving to the table and hopping onto a chair, Alfred folded his hands atop the table's stained surface. The guard motioned for Maggie and her father to get ready to leave. Maggie's father told the guard they needed another moment as she sat in a chair beside him.

"Then I guess I'm stuck here." Her hand enveloped nearly both of his as he looked at her. "Thank you for wanting to help me, Maggie. But like I said there is no changing his mind."

Maggie looked up at her father who told her they only had a minute. Her words seemed to have no sound as Alfred thought of what things would be like without her. Every other patient ignoring him the way they always did; the twirling girls with their patterned footwork giggling at him every time he would shew them off. The boy tapping on the window had even hissed and spat a bloody fingernail at him once. Alfred had to swallow his vomit afterwards when he couldn't find a wastepaper basket.

"There must be something we can do, Alfred," Maggie said as his thoughts sped.

"Me mum may be able to help."

"Then we'll talk to her." Maggie patted his hands before standing. "Don't be givin' up, Alfred."

A coughing fit mixed with a yell meant a third warning. Maggie hugged him just as her father urged her to say goodbye.

"Come, Maggie. Mr. Richards, we'll try to get a hold of your mother if we can. Don't worry. I've dealt with men like your father."

"No man is like him," Alfred mumbled, shaking his head, but he told them his address. And when the common room's doors slammed shut, he thought. *I hope they can, and I hope Maggie's father knows what he's doing.*

The door's lock slid shut as Alfred wearily returned their wave through the door's window. Now all that was left to do was wait, something he was more accustomed to than most. Light faded in and out of the window as the day went on.

Later, when Alfred was being escorted to his room, he wondered if Maggie and her father were heading to his home now. And if so, was his mother there, or had things changed since last, he'd seen her? *With a baby on the way, could it?* He pondered before the door to his cell slammed shut, chasing a plate of food.

He nibbled at the last bit of mush, eyeing every number and image for a third time. They hadn't changed, nor did his mood after swallowing one last bite. Thoughts of what may happen or what he wished would happen stacked in his mind like the books in his bedroom. One pile of the terrible things Charles may do. Another of him seeing his mother again, along with the two friends he'd lost. And the one he had scared away. All of them joined by Maggie at a park, with the sun breaking through the trees.

Pounding on the door, his food disappeared through it. Afternoon came again, joined by the clock tower's chimes, yet for some reason, Alfred didn't find them as bothersome. Maggie's father had been tall, and his jacket sleeves clung tightly to his arms. Alfred surmised that had been from taming the wild and stubborn horses. He imagined his father as an immense, well-kept Clydesdale with a fading blond nose, hooves scratched and chipped, and a roar like thunder. And then Maggie with her hands over her lips, standing close by as her father grabbed the swirling reins. He lay on the bed, closing his eyes, breathing easy at the idea of being home again. His father gone for good with only an hour or so until school started.

The afternoon turned into night as he slept. A breeze blew through the window, drifting to Alfred's nose, *"Koff."* Both eyes opened like corks leaving champagne bottles.

"He is here."

He sat up. The coppery scent of blood was too strong to be a dream. Alfred stared into the darkness and leaned forward, the bedsprings whining the closer his feet came to the floor. The moon's rays made it harder to focus with the pale light streaming into the darkness.

"I see another of my children has decided once again not to keep quiet."

Alfred pressed himself back against the wall. His feet kicked the mattress forward. The voice, like the smell, was too familiar to be mistaken.

"Where...are you? An' what you mean?"

"Your rotund friend will not succeed. And neither shall her father."

The bricks under his bed shook. A crackling like wheels over gravel sounded ahead as the floor split. Light filled the room only for a narrow shadow to ascend the darkened stairs. His father emerged. His fingers clasped the bed's cold metal frame. Instead of a suit, Charles wore long dark robes with the Richards crest atop a chest plate of gold. The light made the serpent-necked dragon twist and turn with each step his father took.

"How could you know 'bout Maggie or anything?"

Charles halted at the top step, leaning forward. His green eyes glowed like those of the creature from his dream shortly after losing Elsa. Alfred's mind questioned if the dream had truly been a dream, or had it had been real?

"It's time you join the others. Come." Charles gestured toward the stairs.

"But how you know about Maggie?" Alfred transfixed himself on his last moments with her, ignoring the mysterious stairs and truths being revealed.

"Always focused on one thing instead of the whole. I own the bloody asylum. Now come, or do I have to force you?"

Alfred leaned left. The stairs led to a hall lined with torches. Gulping, he climbed from the bed and then stood firm. *Jacob was right, and I must be Esa's 'ittle knight.*

"I want to leave this place. Not go where you want. Take me. -"

"Do you not realize what is happening, you miserable fool?" Charles grabbed Alfred by the sleeve. Alfred struggled to pull away, but the claws from his dream dug into his arm. "I should have sent you with her that night."

Pulling and pulling, he gasped before piecing together who his father meant.

"Sent Esa where? She didn't mean to let me fall." He pulled harder, but his father's grip only tightened the farther they descended. Alfred reached for the window above the bed. Dust fell the more the floor rattled. "Answer me. Where you send her?"

Charles threw him down the final six steps, the memory of his fall returning the louder he screamed. Landing on his back, he bumped his head in the same spot. His hands pressed against damp bricks when he tried to stand. Above, the floor was closing faster. Wobbling, Alfred made it to his feet and ran for the stairs only to be blocked by his father.

"You're going where she is and where you have already been." Charles drew a dagger from one of his wide sleeves. The other sleeve almost covered its point, making it wink within the torchlight. "Go now, or must I use force again?"

Alfred turned back to see a door with rounded studs across its surface. Clenching his teeth, Alfred didn't move despite his father's shadow doubling in size from the light. The dagger emerged from the shade of his sleeve like a black serpent with one fang.

"I...won't go. Where that door goes is just a prison." He stiffened his legs, but the blow to the head made them shake. "And if it where you put Esa, let her go too."

His way home was shut, but now neither of them was going anywhere. Charles took a step forward and then back. His face was stone cold like the hall's bricks.

"Stubborn like the others, I see." His father grimaced. "And finally brave? No matter."

Charles pressed a brick on the wall to his left, bringing the door within an inch of Alfred's back. The rush of air knocked him off balance, allowing Charles to snatch his arm again. The door swung open to the dimness of an awakening morning. A gust of wind pressed unevenly against Alfred's face like the surface his hands touched. Alfred turned over when the door slammed shut. Blinking from the wind, he watched the door vanish.

Alfred stood as his mind tried to take in the vagueness of his father's words. The wind pressed the worn grays of his clothes against chest and legs until he found that the ground had run out. He pulled himself back, sending stones clattering over the cliff's edge. The near misstep sent the tiny stones into the clouds below.

"It was real," he gasped.

The village was as it had been in Elsa's stories, its homes surrounded by a wall of stone teeth. Beyond it were miles of forests and fields, except the mountain's height hid the arena. Straight ahead stood the castle, its towers connected by a thick wall, and a vast keep sprang up at the center nearly matching the mountain's height. The R shape of the serpent-like dragon flapped on gold banners above and below diamond windows.

Me family's crest, Alfred thought, yet now he felt as though only his mother resembled that word. Maggie was heading her way and in danger, but when he focused on the village again, he knew Elsa needed him first.

Swallowing, Alfred felt his ears pop. Wind rushed against the back of his head, searching for an easy way down the mountainside. The cold made fending off the dizziness worse. All the while, Alfred tried to channel the courage from facing the Rosekuhs and his father. *The fear of fallin' mustn't stop me.* Yet this was neither a rocking horse nor a flight of stairs.

Finding a climb with plenty of points and edges to grab, Alfred got on his hand and knees and eased down. Each move sent tightness through his arms and legs, making him wince. He wanted to shut his eyes as he had on the stairs at home, but those he knew by number. Wind made it more difficult as it dried his eyes. Sometimes the cracks led sideways while the thin ledges aligned downward. With each agonizing reach, though, the trees below didn't come any closer.

By the sun's position, Alfred knew he had been climbing for minutes. He had read of sundials and the sun's phases. Even with that in mind, finding a ledge nearly as wide as him brought little to no comfort. Panting, a piney scent with hints of maple reached his nose. Looking down, trees of every kind he had dreamed of seeing up close aligned like troops for inspection. The tallest scraped the ledge's coned bottom.

"I'm comin', Esa," he said, swallowing what little spit wasn't dry.

Both legs trembled, and his fingers shook, making each crack or point harder to grasp. Trying to stiffen a leg, he eased it toward the closest and widest cracks. Every few inches added to the previous thousands, making him shake worse. The rock was wet from what might have been a night's rain that the trees had kept moist. Pressing his stomach against the rock face, Alfred felt the pine needles jabbing at his head.

Only what seemed to be a hundred feet remained. Some of his blisters seeped from being torn by the jagged rocks. Moss hid the sharpest like the lips of a green beast. Alfred lowered a hand to one. The moss peeled under his fingers when he moved the other hand, coming off completely as he tried to find the stone under it. But the moss soon gathered between his fingers.

Then a cracking sound came under foot. And then air.

Chapter 6

A constant creaking and the prick of pine needles through his clothes woke him up. Neither annoyance compared to the bombarding pain at the back of his head. Opening his eyes, he found the sun was at its midpoint and was forced to squint. Broken straw scraped against his hand when he rubbed where his head throbbed. Trees gave shade at either side while the mountain's peak looked to be picking at the sun like his fingers were when they found something sticky that had trickled down to his neck.

"Don't pick at it," a deep voice ahead of him said. "Mama said you make it worse when you pick."

Alfred rolled over to see a giant of a boy pulling the cart he was in. The boy was noticeably young in the face, as if he were only fifteen, but his size made him appear older. The fading grays of his tunic revealed parts of his belly where the cloth was belted at his waist. The boy tucked it in with a hand bigger than Alfred's face.

"I go by the name of Leonardo. And you are safe now."

Shuffling through the shoulder deep straw, spots faded in and out every time he blinked. They came in many colors like the flecks of paint on Leonardo's pants.

"Alfred...Richards." Eyeing Leonardo for the club the asylum guards kept at their waist, he saw that a brush was all

that stuck out but kept himself to the cart's rear. "Are we goin'
to the village?

I'm lookin' for someone."

Leonardo sighed as if he sensed Alfred's distrust.

"Si. We are heading in that direction. If there is someone
you search for, he will be there."

Sitting back, Alfred felt the straw crunch under his
bottom. A ruffle through the pile of leaves ahead sent some
fluttering up the sides of the cart. He breathed easy when they
passed under an arch of neatly assembled stonework. Every
time he turned his head though, the motion made him dizzy
and the wooden handles toward the cart's front grew farther
and farther away.

A brief dip from the left wheel rolled him backward,
bumping his head. Dizziness turned to sleep. Straw turned to
static what may have been a question from Leonardo. Deeper
he sank, until his eyelids fell shut and the cart rounded a corner.

"Maggie," Alfred muttered.

His friend came into view from under the trees. Trying
to rise, he felt cobblestones rub against his palms. What was
ahead sent a smile across his lips. *I'm home.* The black of its
front door shortened the more his friend and her father
ascended each step. Maggie raised a thick-fingered hand to
knock as Alfred tried to call her name again. But like the soft
breeze across his face, it came out in a whisper even he could
barely hear. The door opened, revealing someone Alfred was
glad to see, and who was now quite heavy with child.

Josephine spoke softly and properly, as he always
remembered, with words that brought relief.

"My husband is not at home."

Then the door closed just as Maggie's face sank to her chest, making it fluff up a tad.

"We'll find him, dear." Her father gave her a light pat on the back. "And Alfred will be free before we know it."

She nodded as they descended the stairs, but when both touched the sidewalk, a gray smoke shrouded their feet.

"No," Alfred gasped, but again it was so soft.

Footsteps broke his focus on Maggie. Spinning, he saw his father leading a cloud blacker than the shaft of his cane. His green eyes gave the only light in the thickening smoke. Maggie pointed, and her father waved when Charles halted just feet from them. Before Alfred could warn them, the smoke clasped both into darkness, leaving only him and his father.

"Don't worry, Alfred. You shall see your plump friend and her peasant of a father soon." Charles turned around, grinning, swirling the smoke until it formed over the suit he wore.

The street and homes were barely outlines of themselves once the smoke funneled around father and son. Alfred took a step forward, the smoke stinging his eyes. He rubbed them, not understanding how they could hurt in a dream.

"Leave 'em alone!" he yelled.

The smoke spun faster, and Charles's irises disappeared.

"You...what are you?" Alfred's lips trembled when his father's grin revealed pointed teeth.

The stinging increased as did the smell of meat cooking. With a blink to fight it, Charles appeared within inches of him, sending Alfred flat on his back. Alfred twisted and turned to get away. The cobbled stones wrinkled under his palms as he tried to stand.

"They should have left you to be forgotten as I tried. As to what I am, well…" Charles's grin went sour as if what came next was a lemon being bitten too long. "I am one who seeks perfection and yet has not attained it. I am one of many with such a dilemma, and I have searched through time and space to sire a perfect heir to my kingdom."

The swirling smoke increased with the pain engulfing Alfred's head. Charles's words had made it worse, leaving him only with more clues instead of answers. Stiffening his lips, he tried to speak.

"I'll get outta here and save Esa and Maggie. I won't allow you to hurt them no more."

"I truly doubt that." The glow of Charles's eyes dimmed before he turned away.

The smoke rushed into Alfred's nostrils. Blinking and choking, he felt the burning in his throat worsen until his eyes opened to a small fire below a spit. A room formed the more his eyes adjusted. To the right, Leonardo towered over a canvas. The giant popped his head up from it, setting his brush and paints down to turn the meat.

Alfred sat up when Leonardo asked, "How is your head? I followed your…uh…her instructions to the missive. Excuse me. *Letter*, I mean."

Alfred fingered the interwoven bandages around his head. Leonardo was hiding something but not very well. Where the pain was, the bandages felt a little damp.

"I need to find her."

Alfred scooted forward using his hands and feet, struggling among layers of blankets. By the time he made it to the raised pallet's edge, Leonardo was there, his speckled sausage fingers trying to ease Alfred back. The colors on his hands matched those staining his pants. Alfred tried to evade the boy's hands, reaching for the dirt floor, but his captor was quick.

"Patience, piccolo." Leonardo smiled. "We will find the one you seek after you are well."

"Please. Don't call me that." Alfred leaned back and crinkled his nose.

"What?"

"I've read on speakin' Italian. And I know I be 'ittle.'"

Leonardo chuckled, crouching to examine the bandages.

"She said you were smart. I won't call you little. Momma says that my words would get me in trouble."

"Your mother sounds smart like me self." Alfred looked down at his feet and then up, finding Leonardo's touch to be gentle. He leaned forward, allowing the examination to continue. "*Grazie.*"

"Many welcomes to one in need." Leonardo chuckled. This time his belly shook, loosening his tunic. "And now I will make the final touches to the portrait."

Some of the fire's smoke drifted up through a small hole in the ceiling. An open window gave light to Leonardo's canvas, revealing neat mounds of baskets, many of them filled with varieties of vegetables freshly harvested from what Alfred had read of farming. The meat's smoky scent made his mouth water, dripping juices, erasing the pile of mush he had grown accustomed to.

The door to his left opened. Leonardo peered over his shoulder, ceasing his swift brushstrokes. Moving to the woman entering, he leaned toward her, and they whispered. The woman's eyes met Alfred's gaze as a breeze from the door blew her blonde hair. Her face was familiar, yet Alfred felt uncertain. The door eased shut after a final whisper and an assuring nod from her sent Leonardo on his way. Alfred and the woman stared at one another for several seconds, then she moved toward him and sat at his side.

"I'm told you've been looking for somebody." Her eyes scanned the hard work done with the bandages, and then she smiled. "I might be able to help."

With each word she spoke, Alfred wanted to believe she was who he thought her to be. But her lips weren't rosy, and her hair wasn't in a bun. The color of her hair was dirtier, and each lock was tangled, unlike the smoothness it had always been. To follow the many changes—her eyes were red, and crow's-feet numbered in the dozens as if she had not slept in years.

"I believe you 'ready have, though it's hard to believe how fast you did." Tears streamed down his cheeks. "It's been so long. I..." Alfred hugged her.

She returned the embrace with the same care given at the end of every bath and story.

Alfred smiled, sniffing back more tears. And once he focus on her again all the change didn't seem to matter.

"I'm so sorry for wanting to be brave and climbin'—"

"No. Never apologize for wanting to be brave, my little knight." Elsa held him close, careful of his head. "I was heading here whether I did anything or not."

Leaning back while rubbing his eyes, her words didn't make sense.

"Where are we?" he said. "It's like your stories."

Kissing his cheek, she eyed the window's shifting light nervously while her words rushed out. Where they were was just one of many mountains representing many countries.

"The Discarded Lands, we call 'em." Elsa sighed, tears beginning to stream down her face. "We are between the ticks of wished forgotten seconds like the children whose fathers rule the mountains. The fathers wanted them perfect, their dream kids. None ended up so. They sent 'em here—to be forgotten by the world."

To be forgotten is much worse than anythin,' Alfred thought. It was indeed worse than being a dwarf or kept locked away or never making friends.

"Every child, like those wished forgotten seconds, is from other years and places. Expect here, they're stuck as kids, or a young man like you." Elsa smiled a little, rubbing away some of his tears. "You're like the others, their broken dreams," she said bitterly. "Dreams that failed 'em; ones Charles can torture when you sleep."

"But how I see you after father take you?" Alfred said, and then he realized the answer. "I was here in me dream. But how could I be?"

"I haven't the foggiest." Elsa shook her head. "What I do know is...you and the others didn't fail." She grimaced. "Charles didn't give any of you a chance to prove yourselves."

Alfred stared at her blankly. She was not ugly or stupid or fat or poorly spoken like him. Nor was she shorter than most or taller like Leonardo. "Then why did Father send *you* here?"

The door creaked open as Elsa tried to form the right words.

"Elsa, the last of the harvest is done." Leonardo gave a rushed smile toward Alfred. "He wants to see you and your—" Leonardo hushed when he saw Elsa's tears. "Never mind but come *velocemente*."

The door was left wide open, letting in the late afternoon's sun. Elsa returned her focus to Alfred who knew now who she truly was.

"I'm you're...you're me mum."

"Yes, Alfred, I am." Elsa swallowed the last of her sadness, wiping her tears as the two hugged again. "Lets us be joining the others, shall we?"

Alfred nodded as he climbed down from the pallet. They headed down a hill lined on both sides with rows of stoned halls. Fading straw colored their sod roofs. The valleyed mountain, like the high cliff far above, was V shaped. They seemed to align like a stoned creature's gaping mouth. Alfred looked at the people going about their business, noticing subtle similarities to him. *Green eyes and some got blonde hair, too.* His was a gold blonde like his mother, who he wanted to know more.

At near the valley's point stood an entrance with a crowd carrying the mentioned harvest. To either side of its doors stood serpent-like dragons of stone, their necks hunched back in an R shape. A boy with long hair, piercings, a leather jacket, and a demonic band on his shirt spotted them. A great wail or maybe high note, Alfred thought, rang out from the boy's lips, making all turn and part, revealing an elderly man in ice-blue robes.

"The wizard?" Alfred guessed.

Elsa bit her lip, her hand shaking in his for some reason; he could not see why. The wizard was always so wise and strangely spoken in her stories that he'd been Alfred's favorite. The wizard always wore a hood too. Elsa bowed when the wizard turned to them like the others did.

"Ah. So, another of our brothers has joined us from time's normal movement." The wizard pulled back his hood.

"You..., your, the wizard. Mum, what's goin' on?" Alfred thrusted himself in front of her with his fists balled and teeth clenched.

"Be at ease, boy. I am not who you believe. And it appears your mother was unsure to tell you of me." The wizard gave her a look. "Just as she was reluctant for me to go hoodless in her stories."

"Alfred, I'm sorry I didn't tell you. Charles caused you so much pain, and I didn't—" Her words ceased as if someone was choking her.

Alfred looked at her, not knowing what to say. He was still taking in how they were finally together again. Yet a man with a face he hated wore the clothes and spoke in a way he had become fond of as a boy. He kept his back pressed against her even when the wizard smiled before crouching to eye level. The smile was less assuring than his mother's hands that tried to ease his fists loose. Finger by finger loosened only a little, both hands lowering to his hips, but his teeth remained tight.

"Calm yourself," the wizard purred resting his hands on Alfred's. "She is safe, like you, and I would not harm one whom mothered a brother."

It didn't make sense—none of it did. Somehow even with what his mother had said, all of these people, some a little older and some much younger, were all his family. The village was almost something out of the first book Anna had him read. Even the smithy they had passed, with his frog face and bowl cut, was of his blood.

Alfred rubbed his head to sort it out but that pressed the bandages against his wound. He winced, then wrung his wrists instead.

"I believe you," he said when the crowd's whispers worried him, and Elsa nodded assuredly. "By me guess, you be the oldest and first of what father thinks are failures. But you look so much—"

"True again." the wizard said. "However, I am the polar opposite and have tried to raise a champion amongst us to free those who cannot fight."

That's what 'em tourneys were for, Alfred thought as the three moved back to Leonardo's hut. The crowd picked up their baskets and went about shortly after the three were out of ear shot. As they made their way, Alfred took his mother's hand, rubbing it with his thumb until it stopped shaking. The mother he had known his whole life had never needed such comfort, which made him worry for Josephine. *Hope Father don't send her child here too*, he wished before the wizard introduced himself as Mark and said that he had been named after the writer of a most important book.

"Our most recent champion fell to the one of Norway as did many others. Norway's Discarded are free of their mountain as we have tried with great fortitude to achieve."

"Has any of us come close? I remember the tourney from me dream."

They entered the hut once Leonardo had doused the fire, and Elsa's answer was satisfying like his first bite.

"Yes, but Charles pulled you away. I wanted to stop him, but I thought..." Her hand shook again as Mark offered her some meat. She set it aside. "That maybe...he changed. And that he would keep you. It's better up there."

"Mum, he kept me locked in our 'ouse. Just like all of you here."

Elsa made a fist, smirking to look unsurprised, only to bite her lip like before while crossing her arms just as Mark swallowed his fifth bite.

"More have, but we must not dwell on past losses or decisions." Mark patted Elsa's lap. "Now that you both are reunited, we can strive for the first and final victory."

"And I can go back to mama in Rome," Leonardo said.

Mark shook his head, frowning, making his blond-peppered beard sag. Alfred felt the urge to ask why, but his mother spoke first.

"Leonardo, could you take your meat outside?" said the wizard. "And bring your paints too. Paint us something lovely."

Leonardo stood for a moment, swallowed, and then said, "I only know one thing that's *bello*." He grabbed a fresh canvas and his paints from beside his own straw pallet. "This one will be better than the one you seen, Alfred."

The door slammed, sprinkling dust onto the smoldered fire before Alfred realized what he was talking about. "That was his mum an' him in the cell, wasn't it?"

"Yes," Elsa said.

"And neither knows nor shall know of what has become of her," Mark grumbled. "If we can," he continued, sounding optimistic, but only a little bit, "we shall try to return him to a time when she still lived."

Alfred did want to ask how but decided to change the subject. He wanted now more than before to help his mother and, if possible, help Mark return Leonardo to happiness long dead. Something surged in his stomach, the same something that had boiled over against the Rosekuhs. It was desperation mixed with a new something that made him desire to help those he knew and those he may get to know if he did nothing.

I want them free and Leonardo with his mum. Alfred swallowed some of his meat. The spices nipped at his tongue, but what he wanted dulled the taste.

"I'll be the next champion," said Alfred. "Father's taken enough from me an' all us."

Elsa looked at Alfred and then at Mark, who was as surprised as she.

"No, Alfred. The tilts are dangerous." Elsa reached for him. His chair scraped against the dirt floor when she pulled him close. "People die."

The chair was on two legs before he was able to ease himself away.

"Mum...I got to try." He looked up after steading himself. Her face was red and shaky like the night he had fallen from the rocking horse. Then he thought of Maggie. "He got me friend and her father. She is one of the few I got. And she tried to help me in the asylum."

Mark interjected as Elsa took in Alfred's words with begging eyes.

"Then training will aid in this," said the wizard. "I have trained the others in the joust, but..."

Mark stroked his beard for a moment as if he were second-guessing himself. Alfred could kind of see the apprehension from the way the wizard looked at him.

"Mum, Mark, I never had much confidence in me self. But I'm bein' given a chance to. I need to take it."

"Agreed," Mark said. The grin peering through the wizard's beard was not as unsettling this time around. "Elsa, the boy must at this point. After the last tourney, our remaining eldest brethren will not even mount a horse."

Both Alfred and Mark looked at her for many moments. There was a low humming from Leonardo outside the hut. Its tune was the same that Alfred had heard just before his first attempt at bravery:

"Diddle, Diddle, Dumpling, My Son John."

In those seconds to minutes, the moments leading to the door closing surfaced in his mind. Her last words were what he wanted to be for her now.

"You always said I was ya 'ittle knight. And even afta I fell, I wanted to be one." Alfred climbed from the stool and took her hands in his. "Now I can, an' this time it will be for people who need help more than me self."

Elsa looked at him and then toward Mark. Taking a deep breath, she stroked Alfred's hand, then tugged at his soiled asylum clothes. Alfred's heart raced the longer she took. Elsa moved closer to the window, gazing at the moonlight bathing the filled baskets. Eventually she kneeled eye to eye with him and gave a smile and a wink at his worrying face.

"You'll need a change of clothes, my little knight."

Chapter 7

The wind rushed through the trees over a balding field of one of the mountain valley's highest hills. The village's pieced together stonework hid below the trees. Alfred rubbed his fingers, hoping he wouldn't disappoint his brothers and sisters. Mark helped him up onto the horse, giving instructions after catching his breath.

After climbing down the mountain, the horse's height wasn't a challenge. Tremors still ran through Alfred's hands, though. A carriage didn't move unless made to. The horse snorted, pawing at the balding practice ground while Mark applied his armor. It was dinted and almost fit but there was too much room no matter how tight the straps were. Forty yards ahead of him Leonardo moved the quintain into position. A small barn stood to its left and racks of practice lances to the right.

"A few more adjustments shall keep you safe from harm." Mark straightened the small breastplate before double checking the shoulder pads and gauntlets. "You are most lucky that our recent champion was near your size."

Alfred's eyes and mind wandered over to his mother. She weaved her fingers, pulling both elbows into her sides after another breeze came and went. Squinting in the sunlight, Alfred nibbled at his lower lip when she sat on a barrel shaded by a rack of lances. He gave her a wave, not hearing Mark's instructions while trying to give the impression he was okay. The horse moved back and forth between his legs as if replaying the night he fell.

"Alfred, have you been listening?" Mark said.

Alfred blinked, mouth gaping at the flustered wizard in his ice-blue robes.

"I'm sorry. Mum looked worried, an' I just wanted to—"

Mark shoved the helmet into Alfred's hands. A shut and clank from its cone-shaped visor followed.

"She shall be even more so when you fall from Nancy before ever learning to ride her."

As he held the helmet for a moment, Nancy snorted again. The sun glared off the helmet's brow like the ones worn by the knights in his mother's stories. Those knights rode with grace, fearlessly charging and thrusting their lances. A lance lay on the ground behind Mark. It had to be twelve feet in length, and when Leonardo had tried regaining his grip on its rough wood earlier, he'd thought it must weigh a lot too.

"You're right," said Alfred, sighning. "Can you tell me again?"

The wizard narrowed his dark green eyes, making Alfred thrust the helmet on to hide for a second. Mark's eyelids crinkled, and his irises focused just the same as Charles's did. The unyielding focus cracked Alfred's pores like an egg, sending sweat down his face.

"Only once again and with haste, for"—Mark fastened Alfred's helmet to his gorget— "the tourney is a fortnight away."

Mark ran through each item from a full gallop to a trot. Alfred nodded at the end, remembering Don Quixote with his windmills when Mark spoke of how to strike the quintain.

Wobbling with it a little, Mark raised the black lance with its gold corkscrew stripe to him. Tremors ran down Alfred's arm as he tried to hold it upright. The strength Mark displayed made him firm up his grip, so his older brother would not be the only strong man on the mountain. *I don't know if I can do this*, he thought, gripping the reins tighter to assure otherwise. But the lance's weight soon countered any effort once he urged the horse with a spired boot. Nancy bobbed and weaved as his balance did. The lance's point scraped more ground than air the faster he went. At the last minute, he was able to aim it left. "*Scrape*" the shaft went against the quintain's shield. A creaking noise followed when Alfred wheeled the charger around.

"Once more, Alfred!" Mark yelled. "None have made it spin on the first try. Leonardo, set it in place again."

Leonardo wheeled the quintain back into place as Alfred squinted at Mark through the visor's narrow slit. Alfred struggled back to the spot he'd started from, hoping Mark would have more encouragement. But the wizard's face was hard and cold like the visor engulfing Alfred's face. The lance plowed through previously turned earth when he rested it.

He forced himself to cradle the lance under an armpit this time. There was far more control, but the second strike only spun the shield one hundred and eighty degrees. His mother shouted when he returned for a third pass.

"Don't worry, Alfred.," she said. "You'll get it to spin the whole way."

She sounded sure of him like last night, though her face said different. By now, his shaking went from head to toe. The hand holding the reins was losing its strength, and his legs ached from being unable to steady himself. Unlike with rocking horses,' the stirrups were too long for him to reach.

Mark motioned for another go. This time a slap replaced the wizard's anxious grumble.

"What you do that?" Alfred screamed.

The shield came closer this time. Alfred readied the lance, gulping when it was almost leveled. A scrape sent paint flecks flying and the shield spinning the whole way. Alfred grinned, listening for a clap from his mother. His breath bounced off the visor, warming his face the more he tried to slow Nancy to a trot. When he made it back, easing the visor up revealed both Mark and Elsa disappointed.

"It spun the whole way." He pressed the lance's chipped point against the ground. "Isn't that what it's supposed to do?"

Mark scratched his head, looked down and then rested his gaze on Alfred.

"The shield must be struck at the center, and when finally facing an opponent, the chest as well. You will not unhorse anyone or break a lance in any other fashion."

Elsa moved to Mark and whispered. Mark gave a nod, taking the lance in both hands.

"How's a break sound, my little knight?" She unbuckled the first strap on Alfred's breastplate, continuing until his hand stopped her. "We can start when you come back."

"I have to keep goin,' Mum," he said. "Mark said there es 'ittle time."

"Yes, there certainly is." Mark tried to ease his face into a small smile. "I, however, know that with each of our brethren, there are some limitations. Go and walk off the pain you feel. Maybe when refreshed, the shield will be struck true."

Alfred's hands trembled and sweat soaked the pants his mother had given him. He shifted uncomfortably, more from wishing he could help Maggie's and his family than from the forming rash. Staring at his hands again, they shook when he unfastened his helmet. Its black-cloth lining was soaked too. *Maggie would want me to do this right.*

He nodded once the breastplate was off, then groaned when they eased him from the horse. None said a word before Alfred was off and away. The shade from the trees and a light breeze relaxed him a little. Each step was awkward, reminding him of how Maggie walked whenever sweat made raw her inner thighs. They had learned much of each other in the asylum. Some things more personal than needed revealing.

As the gray stones of the village peeked through the trees, Alfred wondered if she and her father were dead. He wonder if Josephine was okay. He wiped the sweat from his brow while doing the same with the thought. Without the sweat running into his eyes, he was able to focus on what he needed to learn upon the hill and on those who depended on him to win in fourteen days.

If ye want something, ye have to try or else why want it at all. Maggies words ran over his mind like the sun's light down his brow. With each step, he worked to decipher a better way to hold the lance. Flexing the stiffness in his thumbs, it popped. He pulled off his gloves, stuffing them in his pockets. The breeze was cool against each digit, soothing their shaking.

Turning up toward the hill, Alfred knew it was strength he needed, and not technique. How to hold it and where to aim was easy. Doubt and pain told him it would take longer than two weeks to get stronger. And tighter fitting armor would help.

Farther down, there was no market and any profession to speak of was the smithy he'd be visiting tomorrow. Three boys were at work, one with horseshoes, another with nails, and a third, the eldest, was the frog-faced boy he'd seen yesterday.

"Hullo," a small, youthful voice said.

Alfred turned around. No one was there. He kept going until a soft thudding started. A quick tug on the sleeve of his gray doublet revealed where the voice came from.

"Hullo, I didn't..."

His greeting pinched his tongue when the little girl waved at him. She grabbed at the two straps holding her satchel with hands blacker than his boots.

"I'm the village's personal historian." She reached up with one hand to shake his, holding herself upright with the other. "Mark said we had a new brother. I'm Emily."

The urge not to cry or be the least bit awkward battled for supremacy when Alfred shook her hand. Her smile was bright like her dress, matching the color of Mark's robes.

"I like yer dress." *Father, she so young and has no...*

"Thank you. Don't worry, Alfred" She giggled. "We're all used to staring."

He blinked, realizing he had been at what was missing, the things which ached him now.

"I'm sorry. So, you're the village's historian an' all?" *I need to get back up there. Now more 'an ever. But why am I—* Alfred wanted to ask her how she had gotten the dress. Instead, he said, "You want to come up an' watch me train? Bet I'm the first dwarf to do it."

Emily giggled again as Alfred led her up the hill, though what was funny, he could not tell. He hated it when the boys back at school stared. When halfway up the hill, his answer to what would have been an unnecessary question was answered.

"Did Mark make your doublet? He is so wonderful. He's actually the village's priest and seamstress, but most of us call him—" She stopped suddenly, hiking up her satchel as if the name was too soon. "Well, you will maybe. If you win the tourney instead, we can see the Beatles when I go home."

"Beatles?" Alfred said. "We can do that lookin' under the bushes."

"Oh, sorry," Emily said. "I'm from the sixties. You must be from earlier. They're a music band and totally groovy."

"I'd like to hear a song. You know any?"

They were near the hill's crest before both were smiling and Emily had finished singing "From Me to You."

Some of Alfred's pain was gone, more so thanks to one he believed was a new friend. The joy was trampled by the loud thuds Leonardo's feet made as he ran up to them.

"*Per favore*, *per favore*, tell me you are continuing your training, piccolo," begged Leonardo, huffing and puffing, bending over to catch his breath. "I am far too frightened to mount a horse, and don't want to hurt Nancy with my great weight."

"What you talking about?" Alfred said. "I'm not quitting. Who said anythin—"

"No one has." Mark came up behind Leonardo, joined by Elsa. "We only sent him away for a brief reprieve."

Doubt budded in the wizard's eyes, and for the first time, Alfred was the one needing to give assurance, though it felt strange.

"I know what me problem is an' me new friend here helped solve it."

Emily, Mark, and Elsa looked at him confused, yet better that than doubtful.

"She has more muscle in her arms than I, thanks to what she doesn't got. Along with the trainin', I'll climb up the hill just with me arms and hands."

Both Mark and Emily and even his mother smiled when they heard the idea. Leonardo sighed with relief, giving a pat on Alfred's back, and almost knocking him on his face. Alfred took a deep breath, trying his best not to get angry at the giant's overzealousness. Leonardo was so excited he hopped around in a circle, dropping brushes from his pockets.

"That is most *bene*," said Leonardo. "And as a reward, I paint you something special on your shield."

They watched the giant run down the hill, forgetting his brushes for a moment, and then running back to get them. Alfred and Emily followed Elsa and Mark to the practice ground. This time, Alfred believed things would get better, and as he made pass after pass, Emily recorded his journey to the Discarded Lands, most of which Alfred had told his mother yesterday and she happily shared with Emily. Panting after a third pass, Alfred saw Mark's eyes ease and his lips relax, leading Alfred to hope, though the visor made it difficult to be sure.

Later, as the sun dipped into the west, the mountain resembled a beast with diamonds on its tongue from each hut lighting its cookfires. The four of them gathered in one nearest the dragon-guarded gates. It was the most spacious of any, with rows of pews on both sides and an isle leading to a dais chiseled from the mountains' lower right canine. There Alfred sat beside Emily as Mark grilled some vegetables over a fire pit at the center of the dais.

His body ached, but the smell made it easier to manage. Elsa gave the vegetables a turn on each of their spits. Something Emily had said earlier peaked in Alfred's mind. She was nearly through the lyrics of another Beatles song, when he asked, "What you mean I'd be callin' Mark something, Emily?"

Emily forced down a swallow, setting her plate aside while both her words and dinner struggled in her throat. Mark interjected before the little scribe could answer.

"No need to bother with such things. I am most fascinated by your idea of earlier. To think of what you wish to do to improve is most—"

"Mark," Elsa said. "It's not something to be ashamed of. You have done so much for all of us, and should Alfred—"

"What es it?" Alfred barked. His curiosity foamed to frustration. Standing, he almost lost his balance, but Emily grabbed his pant leg.

"We call him Father," said Emily. "And he's been so good to every one of us. He was there when we were hurt, scared, hungry, or sick. We owe him a lot."

"That is why I call him a wizard in my stories, Alfred." Elsa smiled. "And I got faith that you will win."

Alfred moved to the dais's top step. Looking over the pews, he noticed it was like a makeshift church. He had never been to church yet knew every chapter and verse of the Bible thanks to Anna. He'd also never had a real father either. *He looks a lot like the father who put us here. How could they?* Alfred turned back to the wizard. His eyes were gentle, not stern. Instead of tight, disgusted lips, or a tormenting grin, both were light and loose with concern. More than anything else, Emily and his mother were at ease around him. A trust not found with Charles emitted from the man arranging him a plate.

"I'm sorry for getting mad like that. I will win, like you said, Mum, with all ya help."

They returned to the grilled vegetables. The fire crackled almost as if in applause at more of Emily's songs. Alfred's grilled onion snapped when he bit into it—after, of course, he had bowed his head with the others while Mark led everyone in prayer. When the meal was done, Alfred's eyes grew heavy, almost shutting. The makeshift church's door creaked open.

Mark raised a finger to his lips and whispered, "Rest easy tonight, Alfred. We have much to accomplish in so little time."

"Where you goin'?" Alfred mumbled. "You got to sleep, too."

Mark gave him a small smile, blinking with heavier eyelids than Alfred's. "My night does not end until all I know are well and in bed."

He really es a wizard. Alfred smiled.

"Good night then."

The door eased shut at the moment Alfred's eyelids did.

Morning broke earlier than Alfred expected. A rooster crowed, and something nudged him from the warmth of his blanket. Mark handed him an apple, which he bit into while sitting up. Alfred leaned back, finding he had rolled in his sleep to near the dais's edge.

"Come, Alfred, all are already up, and you have a hill to climb."

Alfred pulled on his boots, noticing Emily and his mother were gone, their blankets folded in neat piles. Mark pushed open the doors, breathing noises into Alfred's waking ears. Cartwheels whined, smithy hammers tinged, and the youngest of his siblings sat in a circle around Emily. She waved at him as he tried to keep pace with Mark. The children around Emily sat in the laps of women his mother's age and younger. The waving and shaping of her blackened hands told him she was in the midst of a story. Alfred caught up to Mark as the women and children grew small from distance. *I hope Josephine don't 'ave to join 'em with her baby.*

"Them women holding them little kids," Alfred said, gesturing to them with his chin. "Who are they?"

Mark halted short of the trees once Alfred had passed under the arch. The wizard breathed deep, rubbing his worn fingers.

"They are mothers who brought our father more disappointment. The children were expected to die, from how ill they appeared. Because of their mother's love, they were sent here, mother and child to be spared. This place can halt illness—one of the few advantages to being trapped between the ticks of a second."

Alfred got on his hands and knees, ready to climb the hill as planned. He still wanted to know how his brothers and sisters and their mothers had truly survived. Gripping the dirt, he steadied himself.

"Why did Father not kill them? I know it cruel to ask, but I don't understand how any of us are really here."

"That is an answer for the evening," Mark said. Ascending the hill, his shoulders slumped as if both carried a heavy load meant to drag him down.

"Please tell me."

The wrinkles under Mark's eyes resembled decades of worry to Alfred.

"He has killed some." Mark sighed. "The ones among us—along with those who have tried to win our freedom—showed what those dead didn't: courage."

Breathing deep, Alfred felt a sense of pride in knowing he had done the same. One hand followed the other. He let his legs go limp. His pace stayed steady for several yards until the hill's steepness made his arms bow a little. The stabbing of stones grew worse farther up. He groaned with each agonizing reach, wanting to rest. Remembering the sadness in Mark's voice earlier, he knew he could not allow any time for rest. Pebbles stuck painfully to his palms. He shook them off or clawed at patches of grass to wipe them away.

Once his fingers clasped the crest of the hill, Mark had just rest the saddle on Nancy and was tightening the saddle cinch. The armor of yesterday rested over a newer lance. Alfred didn't know if he could hold a lance—or, for that matter, stand to wear the armor again. His arms shook as if they were about to fall off and crawl away into the bushes.

"You may visit Albert, Robert, and Christopher after a few passes. They worked day and night on better-fitting armor and helm for you," Mark said as Alfred stared at the armor.

Alfred's stomach barely brushed the curve of breastplate after it was securely fastened. Even after the time spent applying the armor, he was still winded from the climb. Smaller armor would make every pass to come less like living in a bucket. His hands shook worse, but he hoped that with practice there would follow stability.

Pass after pass sped the time faster. The sun was at its midpoint, and Alfred's helmet was filled with sweat like water in the pitchers from school—the ones that had spilled over the day he'd fought the Rosekuhs. He pulled the helmet off, wishing it had been filled with cool water instead of sticky sweat.

Alfred went down the hill to see the brothers. After a hundred yards he was greeted by a boy who came out from among the heat and smoke of the smithy shop.

"Hello there! How can I help you?"

"Christopher, what did we tell you?"

The pointy-jawed boy with his welcoming eyes turned back as a taller boy thrust a glowing nail into a bucket. It hissed as he took two steps toward them in his gray shorts and apron.

"Stop greeting everyone when they come by. And get back to work."

Christopher turned back to Alfred, unmoved by the taller boy's rude tone, and then said with the same welcoming smile, "Hello there! How can I help you?"

"I came to see how me armor is goin'," Alfred said leaning back after Christopher repeated his greeting. "Mark said you three are best of all the mountain smithies."

Christopher nodded in a fast motion with each word. Then, almost as if Alfred had just arrived, the boy blinked and repeated himself a third time. The taller boy came over, took Christopher by the hand, and jerked his head to where frog-faced boy was. Seconds later, the frog-faced boy stopped stoking the fire to shake Alfred's hand.

"I'm Albert, and Robert is almost done with the helmet's visor. Should fit better than the one you have."

Older helmets, breastplates, and various other pieces of armor hung along the walls. They were polished but dented, and some had holes through their chests. Robert rested an old gauntlet in the fire as Christopher stoked it. As smoke rose and the gauntlet glowed, Alfred admired the way the heat melted what was once solid. Christopher spotted him and was about to go to greet him again, when Robert pointed, cursed, and then told Albert to speed things along so Christopher wouldn't get distracted for the millionth time.

"Please excuse those two, Alfred. One has no cork to plug his mouth, and the other, well... He has a truly short memory. Twenty seconds, to be exact."

"That okay," said Alfred. "How the rest of me armor goin'?"

Albert guided him to a table in front of a pile of scrap metal. The frog-faced boy looked at it, shaking his head before presenting a pair of gauntlets, knee pads, and stirrups with shorter straps.

The shorter straps attached to stirrups sent a relief to Alfred's legs, but Albert's chin sank, making Alfred curious.

"What wrong? They look like the nice ones on the wall."

"They do, don't they? Masterpieces everyone. I just hope this new one doesn't need melted down with the pile over there. The others I just couldn't part with, and some the boys made themselves."

The pieces on the table shined with no burrs or sharp edges. Picking up one of the knee pads, Alfred ran his fingers across its curved shape. Two days were near done, and he was no stronger. He placed it back on the table.

"I won't let that happen."

"Thank you," Albert said.

Alfred smiled at him, ignoring the way his hand shook before resting it on Albert's back. What little chin Albert had merged with his neck. "I'll keep the boys working like always. You may be a little fellow, but I think that may give you an advantage."

"Why's that?"

Albert's smile widened. "Easy to hit someone big. Small, though, now that's tricky."

Chapter 8

Every unevenly chiseled step was wet from last night's rain. They hugged the mountainside and were narrow, making the chattering of his teeth louder than his thoughts. Even with the finished armor and the layers underneath, Alfred was no warmer and no less nervous. The arena was larger than he remembered, and the mountain's crisscrossing stairs made it seem even larger the lower he went. Alfred walked along a wide, leafy path that had already been trampled by his siblings ahead of him.

Outside the champion's entrance, banners moved in the wind like autumn leaves on trees. Instead of a leafy smell, like the changing trees at the mountain's base, another smell drifted from the arena—that of horse manure, which mated with the buzzing of flies. Unlike the smell of blood, which he braced himself for, it didn't make him nauseous.

Alfred double-checked the straps on his gauntlets. The leather whined, confirming what he had done a dozen times already. Above the stall where Nancy stood was the Richards crest. Colorful banners brightened the other stalls, but this was etched into the wood by hand. Hearing heavy, fast-paced footfalls, Alfred hoped Maggie and Josephine still lived. Frowning, he turned around. His face found itself inches from a shield.

"Do you like it?" Leonardo said. "I just finished it."

Its gray background resembled a cliff's face with a man gripping with one hand while reaching downward. The man was small, dressed all in gray, but the clothes had been made to look like armor. His hair was blowing back, revealing a determined look. *It me climbin' down when I got here.* Alfred wasn't sure what to say. All the other knights had the crests of their mountains atop of theirs. The careful detailing of the armor and his face made the R-shaped dragon over the stall look like a worm with teeth. Then the question peaked when Leonardo shoved it into his hands.

"I like it," he said. "Guess you saw me up there?"

"Everyone did." Leonardo chuckled. "Nobody who has come here has made it down without breaking a bone. You be a very sturdy little fellow—oops, just fellow."

Alfred fell silent for a moment, feeling a sense of resilience. The clopping and creaking of boards above them sped up his nerves again. Mark and Elsa appeared from behind Leonardo as Alfred slid the shield's straps over his left arm. Mark gave him a nod and wink before sending the giant to take his seat. Then, with a pat on his shoulder, the wizard placed Alfred's helmet beside the horse and readied it. His mother caught his eye, dressed the same as in the dream. Now, though, he knew that it had been real. Her hair was brushed and without any tangles, and her rosy lips were back.

"I want you to know that"—she knelt and looked into his eyes, drawing her lips inward. "I'm prouder of you than anyone can possibly know. And though we were apart for so long, I—"

Alfred hugged her, careful of his breastplate and shoulder pads. The sun peeked between the slow-filling seats above. Her shoulders shook, and her tears tapped on the plates covering his boots. He covered her with his shield from the onlookers passing by. They returned to their tasks at hand, sensing what Alfred didn't use to. He had been almost shunned from all emotion or comfort for twelve years. Even Gwen had been forced to keep her care for him a secret.

"Mum, I promise." He whispered. "I promise you won't lose me again."

She looked up from his shoulder, kissed his cheek, and rubbed the remnants of her lipstick away. He stopped her thumb just short of erasing it entirely.

"I will free us." He looked around at the other boys, wanting to say they didn't look so bad, but he couldn't lie. "They may be big." Alfred grinned, "but I'm small and tricky to hit."

Elsa laughed, rubbing her tears on the gray of her sleeve. "You certainly are my little knight."

Rising, his mother went to join Leonardo. Alfred turned to find Mark. The wizard's face was blank of emotion. Alfred picked up his helmet, shaking the straw off. The wizard's robes narrowed into a thin slit of color through the visor.

"All is set for the day," said Mark. "Are you ready?"

Alfred sighed, raising both arms. Wet mud dropped from his boots as Mark helped him into the saddle. The stalls were dark with only the burning sconces to break up the night they produced. Mark rested his hand on Alfred's leg, giving it a reassuring squeeze.

"I'm proud of you, too."

He rubbed his fingers. A small smile and another sigh made the little holes in Alfred's visor hum. Mark did as the others, leading their champions out onto the field. Alfred thought the lists would be torn up from age. Instead, fresh grass—wet from the night's storm—ran along a fence, keeping the eager spectators at bay. The lists had neatly raked white sand with spots still brown from the rain. The Russia's bear clawed and roared on at least a dozen red banners. Below, the discarded were almost beastlike. Another symbol displayed was that of the South American black jaguar. Mark had said their father was rumored to be an exiled Incan prince, who later conquered the whole continent—all before he bent the Spaniards to his will to do it.

Many other banners appeared to be just as unique, including one that Alfred hadn't been told about. Yet no other inspired bravery over fear. *America.* he thought. The eagle made it obvious, but the children below were deformed in no way he could tell. All were a mix of the others, but everyone wore their own clothes, unlike the plain grays, blues, and blacks.

Once all champions were in a line, trumpets sounded, sending everyone's eyes to an immense viewing stand. All went silent as ten men, dressed in clothes Alfred recognized from the books of his father's study, sat down. Alfred's eyes widened within the dark of his helmet when each face was that of every drawing and photo too. The one of the Incan prince, with his feathered crown, long, dark hair, and painted face was exact. Then, when Mark handed him the reins, Alfred's hand tightened so fast that Mark needed to grab his leg again.

"Don't." Mark hissed.

The wizard's hand pinched close to Alfred's knee. It loosened only when a woman, heavy with child, followed in behind Charles.

"You shall give father and those in his company satisfaction."

"What?" Alfred said. "Let go. He got Maggie, an' her father, an' Josephine."

"I know. But if you act out, he will have a victory before the tourney begins. And you may endanger another of our brethren."

"I won't. And he's not gonna to hurt what could be his chance at his dream child."

Alfred shoved Mark's hand away, guiding his charger forward until her hooves were an inch from the list wall. Lifting his visor, the Russian mountain lord in his layered furs pointed a hairy finger, making Charles and Josephine turn from their conversation.

"Alfred." Charles's eyes flashed a hint of surprise in a stew of anger. "Leonardo was meant to represent your brethren." His jaw stiffened while searching for Leonardo. "Where is the coward?"

"Leave him alone, Father. He painted me shield. Now where you got Maggie and her father?"

Charles narrowed his eyes, smirking before giving up the search and returning to his seat. Josephine turned up her nose at Alfred, but the more she did, the more her lips trembled.

"I said you would see them again," said Charles. "I keep my word unlike you and that Italian mammoth."

Charles waved a hand, and large doors to Alfred's right rumbled open pushed by men bigger than Leonardo. They stood guard, faceless with their visors down. Clydesdales snorted, pulling a cart topped by a cage of iron bars. Children above held their noses when the shadows slid back like a stage curtain.

"No," Alfred gasped.

Maggie lay motionless, straw forming a jagged beach around her. Her father's body formed an X on her pale skin like one found on a treasure map. Alfred urged Nancy with quick, spurring jabs. The pounding of hooves muffled Mark's calls for Alfred to come back. Maggie was naked, and excrement dripped from the cart. It left a trail from the doors, pooling when the driver was ordered to halt.

Alfred yanked off his helmet, tears welling up in his eyes. He let the helmet hang by his fingertips. It made a scraping sound against his shield when he reached for her. Maggie's hands were bound to the bars at both sides. He shook one, calling her name until laughter crept into his reddening ears. Alfred let her hand go, looking down. His heart raced from how high he was.

Another dripping sound sent his eyes to a large, bloody gash in her father's stomach. The breakfast of just five hours earlier surged. Alfred shook his head, trying to hold back dead fears and the foul taste on his tongue. *"If ye want something, Alfred, ye have to try. Or else, why want it at all."*

He swallowed, thrusting his helmet on—this time not in fear, but to muffle the rage growing louder. It exploded as his heavy breathing sent warm air against his face. Alfred raced toward the laughter, glimpsing the faces of fellow Discarded. Some were nearly as angry as he, but they sat still, not wanting the metallic guards to notice. Others were in tears by the time he was face-to-face with Charles.

His father rose to the railing of the viewing stand, meeting Alfred outside a lance's reach. The sun bounced off his visor, onto the golden dragon of Charles's breastplate as he raised it. Alfred glared up at his father.

"Why?" he said, gnashing his teeth. "They just want to help me, and you slaughtered them."

Charles's grin morphed. His skin turned scaly until it matched the gold of his breastplate. His eyes glowed, matching their brightness with the rumbling growl in his throat.

"They gave you hope. And hope shall not be allowed to fester in those who failed me."

Alfred swallowed again, this time to hold back any wish—any wish that would or could risk the family he'd always wanted, the mother he barely knew, the one he did, and the sister whose singing kept him going in the days leading to this one.

"You like deals, Father? Got one a Richards can't refuse to honor."

Charles leaned back, breathing wisps of black smoke, letting them fade.

"I'm listening."

"When I win, you let me, my mums, and the others go free."

Charles rolled his eyes, arching his tongue through his pointed teeth, ready to laugh again.

"What use are my recent wives to a boy like you?" he said. "And can you muster a deal I have not already—"

"Shut up," Alfred growled. A flicker of green sent sparks from his eyes to the back of his helmet. Charles recoiled, but only a little, snarling as Alfred seethed. "When I win, everybody goes free."

A roar surged from the other mountain lords. Faces, aged slightly by time, morphed into dragons of other-colored scales—some with large horns, others with long snouts, and a few with long, thin mustaches.

"Silence, all of you," Charles roared, turning to them.

Alfred smiled a little when Josephine did.

"Don't be fools. He will lose as big as he is small." Charles turned back to Alfred after the smile Josephine had given vanished. His father's grin returned, but wider thanks to his pointed teeth. "Isn't that right, Alfred? Just the same with my butcher shop; only this time, death will be the choice of punishment."

"I doubt it," Alfred said.

He galloped back to Mark and the other champions, listening for what he thought would be more silence. Instead, the arena grew so loud with cheers the wind couldn't be heard. Tears from just moments ago made way for smiles. Hands clapped at the speed his horse galloped. The champions, masked by multi-shaped visors, raised them in wonder. Alfred ignored them, hoping for some reason despite their common goal that they would still fight. Mark took Alfred's reins when the first two champions were called forth.

The wizard helped him down, tying off the reins he'd taken from Alfred. Alfred, like the others, stood on the sidelines as heralds announced Japan and Thailand.

"That was both brave and foolish." Mark paused, scratching his chin. "But, with any luck, it will thin the competition."

"I don't want it easy," Alfred said. "A mountain's goin' free no matter what. But if I beat 'em all, an' Father, they will all win for once."

With his visor raised, Alfred saw pride carving itself across Mark's face. Somehow it made a man, aged by parenthood return to youth for a moment. Alfred and Mark shared a common love of books. Mark's books were mostly fiction, ones that would exist many years beyond Alfred's own time. A lance cracked against a shield, breaking, making Alfred jump a little from his trance. *Five points already. I didn't think it go this fast.*

He raised both hands to lean on the single-bar fence as the others did. When the two champions readied again, he thought of the hero dressed like a bat, and the one Mark called the Man of Steel, of how—no matter the opponent—both always found a way. One used fear and planning, and the other inspired courage using strength.

Crack went another lance, but this time more than a lance broke. The boy of Thailand with his white leg bands and armbands fell to the ground. Sand kicked up before the boy could think. And then the Japanese boy dismounted to finish the job. Alfred knew this sometimes happened. He tried to resist the urge to run out and stop the falling katana. Blood pooled in a sun shape on the white sand as the boy of Japan let out a victory cry, making Alfred's ears ring. He closed his eyes for a second, hoping nobody would expect this from him.

The faceless guards removed the boy's body while the boy of Japan claimed the Thai horse for a prize. When the screaming ceased, Alfred's ears stopped ringing and his fear subsided. Fortunately, there were two more before him, giving time to gather his wits.

Alfred pulled off his helmet to wipe the sweat away. After a second swipe, he looked at the cage. One by one, turkey vultures appeared high above. They landed, squawking, snapping at each other and poking their scrawny heads between the bars. A few continued circling while a large one nibbled away at Maggie's father's fingers. Alfred shook his head to refocus on the two champions. It wasn't long until the Portuguese champion made the Irish one reel in his saddle.

The two were about to go again when Josephine caught Alfred's eye. Her lips curled while she turned her nose up to look unimpressed by the skill of the first four boys. Sipping from her chalice, her eyes could not hide her worry from him. *I may have me real mum back, but she needs me too.* Alfred thought, returning his focus to the knights. Five points thanks to a broken lance gave Ireland the lead. Josephine stayed still. Alfred found himself giving her an assuring nod as something nudged his shoulder.

"Come, we must ready you, Alfred," said Mark. "This match is near its end."

"But they at five to one now," Alfred answered, following the drift of the wizard's wintery robes.

"Not for much longer."

Mark was spot on. The match ended when both made it to the lance rack. Alfred flew upward until Mark had him high enough to swing his legs into place. The Portuguese knight fell, reaching for the list, leaving claw marks in the wood. Nancy snorted after Alfred secured his gorget to his helmet. There was no scream this time, or the iron-like smell of blood like before. Instead, bagpipes filled the air, making Alfred's helmet hum and rattle from the tune.

Mark readied a lance when the music was hushed by roars. Alfred's mouth gaped. His lance felt heavier than the first time he'd held one. He couldn't tell if she was really a bear, or just poorly groomed. The Russian champion wheeled her large shoulders, stretching her tree-trunk arms—and she was tall. Alfred held his lance at the ready. His opponent's squire had to climb a ladder just to screw on her elongated visor. Fur pressed out from it like a shoe stepping on grass.

"Hullo, Alfred." Emily hopped up next to him just as a boy in a red, double-breasted doublet skipped out. He announced the Russian girl as Emily cleared her throat.

"Soo, how do you want me to announce you?" she said. "I was going to sing something, but I figured it wouldn't be scary enough."

The quick pace of her voice broke the dry film forming over his eyes. Alfred had begun to wonder how what Mark *said* happened *could* happen. He looked at Emily in her ice-blue dress, trying to decide what she should say. Then he remembered what Leonardo had said earlier and the way it had filled him with confidence after hearing it.

"Call me Alfred the Sturdy. The Little Knight and... No, it stupid."

"I like the first two." Emily smiled. She yanked out a paper and pencil to record it for later. "Come on. I'm sure it will be grrrrreat."

Alfred liked it when she referenced characters from her time, and she'd told him all about the cereal tiger. That one he wanted to use but decided on something else.

"The Climber of Mountains." He suggested.

Emily's eyes popped like awakening stars. Her lips went wide as she clapped.

"That is so groovy," she said. "It goes with your shield and was so neat to watch."

"You best go, Emily," Mark said. "The young man has just finished."

Alfred waved, thanking Emily as she cleared her throat again. Her voice hinted at the wish to turn the words into song. To Alfred, it was almost as if she had, for when she had finished, the crowd cheered. He slid his visor shut just as the trumpet sounded. The crowd's excitement rose and fell with each forgotten foot. Alfred lowered his lance, using all that he had learned in one smooth motion. His arms didn't shake and both hands gripped evenly. The lance lowered to proper height.

A rush of air made his straps flap when his lance struck her shield. Vibrations ran up the shaft into his arm, followed by a cracking. He pointed the lance up to start again. Alfred thought he'd broken a lance, but only a point was gained. His heart sank, but then rose a little. He knew he was winning, but a broken lance would have hastened things. Alfred looked at Charles. He couldn't tell if his father was nervous or angry.

Charles was gripping the arms of his chair tightly. Sweat ran down his face, but his teeth were clenched as if ready to attack. His face, like the faces of the others, was back to human form. Except the others were sinking back into their chairs. Alfred didn't know what scared them more. Charles or that Alfred was winning.

It was barely a minute before the strength of the Russian girl matched her size. Alfred gasped, dropping his lance. He raised his visor, swiping his hands across his left side to feel for a broken point in his stomach. But his brother's armor had held. Only a can-sized dent needed pounding out, and Mark was ready to hammer it.

"Are you well, Alfred?" Mark loosened the breastplate's straps. "I wasn't sure the rumors of bear's blood were of truth but—"

"They are," Alfred said, panting. "She hit me again, I be on me back."

The pinging gave him a headache the faster Mark hammered. Reattaching the breastplate slowly, they both shudder when the Russian girl unscrewed her visor and flashed her long canines.

"Then you must use the shield as it is meant to be, should she strike again. She is more—"

"I know, Mark. Please, I'm not fast enough."

"Then be so," Mark barked. "Or you shall be dead like that poor—"

Dry coughs forced themselves out of Mark's lips, reddening his cheeks as he gasped for further words. Alfred wasn't sure when the last strap was fastened if Mark was going to be okay. He looked at his opponent, then to the herald ready to signal another go. His mind spun, thinking of how bathing in bear's blood could have birthed a girl so huge. And since Charles was truly a dragon, would he be even stronger yet? But he had to win and needed Mark to do it.

"I'll go fast enough. I'll use the shield." He rested a hand on Mark's shoulder just as the wizard struggled to hand him another lance. "Please be okay. I need you."

The wizard rubbed his eyes, smiling faintly. "I promise."

The two opponents went again. Alfred adjusted his shield just as Mark had shown him. Readying the lance, he pretended the cliff face on his shield was the real one he climbed. And with a thrust, wood split, and the crowd went silent.

Chapter 9

I t was so high, so quick, that not even Alfred was sure it had happened. The sand kicked up so much and so fast that it looked as if the Russian had dug her own grave. Only the powdery thuds of her horse's hooves were able to break the trance all were in. Alfred raised himself a bit in his stirrups, leaning to the left, hoping she wasn't dead. Her father roared from behind Charles as silence broke into whispers.

When two guards grabbed her under her arms and legs, she let out a low chuckle. It sounded wet and guttural, like water struggling through a dirty downspout. Alfred breathed easy just as the Discarded cheered, then he returned to Mark. The wizard's color was normal, and a chuckle shook the strands of his beard.

"A congratulation is in order, Alfred," said Mark. "That was the first lance anyone of our family has broken in some time."

Mark took the spent lance from Alfred. When he was about to ask how Mark was feeling, the cheering was broken by a slow clapping. Alfred turned his horse, raising his visor to what could have been a mocker's chance.

"Well, it appears my most recent disappointment has more spirit than previously thought. Good show, Alfred." Charles's callused hands formed fists. He crossed his arms making his robes appear as a black serpent wrapping itself around his wide chest. "Luck will only come once. Do not expect it to continue."

Alfred returned his attention to Mark as the next champion he'd face readied. Mark slid a fresh lance from the rack, halting before hoisting it up.

"There is no such thing as luck, Alfred," his brother said. "One makes their efforts a success. We have many to face before father climbs off his high seat. And then, you will keep him down."

Flexing his fingers for a moment, his brother's words didn't make sense at first. And then slowly Alfred pieced them together like they were the stonework of the mountain village. It was he who'd chosen not to be alone in the asylum. Him who had found courage as the floor split open, and he that had stood up to the one man he had feared most. Finally, with a friend's life at stake and the chance to rescue another, Alfred had made the climb down the mountain.

"Then I'm gonna make me self win an' free us all."

Mark's smile grew like Alfred's confidence. Emily raised her hands, chanting the words from before so loudly that it was as if she thought they would part the sleepy clouds above. At the far side of the arena, a boy with red, white, and blue feathers pluming from his helmet smiled. The boy slammed his visor shut. It was crafted to match the shape and curved point of an eagle's beak.

The crowd's spirits rose, seconds passed, and the clouds slowly parted. Emily waved her hands in the air as if her wish had been granted. "*Crack*" went the American boy's lance, bouncing off Alfred's shield. Alfred squeeze his legs tight against the horse's sides. Nancy let out shrill scream when his spurs dug and pinched her flesh. Alfred shook his head and gasped. He was no longer on the mountain of his shield. A jagged scratch had split the entirety of the image in two, making it appear as if the lance had broken away the cliff face.

"My portrait," Leonardo yelled.

The giant burst into tears. Alfred's mother rubbed Leonardo's hand to comfort him. Leonardo deep rumbling cries filled Alfred's throat with emotion. He hope when all was over his brother could paint the same portrait. The detail was far to intricate to be left damaged. Across the way, cackles erupted behind Charles, who almost choked when sipping his wine. Purple ran into the fading blondes of his beard, turning it red. Alfred ignored the almost booming-like laughter pouring from his father's lips.

He went back to his starting point, griping his lance tightly, trying to ignore the mountain lords laughter. Mark grabbed hold of Nancy's bridle, stroking her neck. Alfred's eyes stung the same as they had done from earlier. He yanked his helmet off and rub them, but the burning only settled a little. He covered his face, lowering the lance. Tears rolled from eyes the more they burned and having his father notice would make things worse.

Finally, Alfred loosened his legs, allowing Mark to fully calm the panicking horse. His lance was still intact, but the American boy's was broken. Panic wanted to settle in, and an ache begged for rest from his shield arm. He shrugged off the pain knowing too many depended on him.

Readying the lance, the rabble mountain lords continued to burrow through the steel of his helmet. Only one thing, Alfred thought, would make his brother happy and stop the mockery from those in his father's viewing stand. *This one, an' five more.* Peering over to the still-amused mountain lords, he gave his charger a kick. The American boy looked up and spat. He screamed for a lance, forgetting his visor. He sent his mare barreling forward. Noticing his shield wasn't in the right place, Alfred thrusted.

Alfred's lance point punched through plate, sticking in place. It snapped from the force of both of them heading opposite ways. Blood spewed from the boy's lips, darkening his already black skin. His blood phased to a bright scarlet as it dripped from his chin. The boy fell from his horsed and struck the sand with a metallic thud. The crowd's excitement outran the pace of Alfred's heart. Tears welled up in his eyes once again, forcing him to turn away. What Alfred hadn't wanted to happen, had. Looking at his father, he expected to see worry, but there was none. There was pride. Something Alfred himself thought he should feel but didn't want to.

"How many?" Alfred asked, returning to his starting point.

Mark looked at him confused. Sweat and tears ran into Alfred's trembling lips as he unfastened his gorget and yanked his helmet off.

"How many of us have to die or got to kill just to be free?"

The wizard's eyes fell to the ground. Mark looked up drawing in a deep unsettling breath.

"Hundreds." Mark said, finally. "Eternally young but not immortal, those little ones you saw, safe from their previous ailment, will die from the coming winter cold."

Wheeling around to the American boy, Alfred's mind drifted back to the Thai boy, fast-forwarding to a victory he hoped for. *Could I do the same to father?*

"Killing comes in a man's life, Alfred, whether in service to his own country or by ill choice in solving a problem."

"I don't want to kill again, Mark." Alfred sighed.

"Good." Mark smiled. "Then you are the hero I see you to be." Mark's face went dark for a moment, as if he were second-guessing himself, making Alfred unsure of his brothers' faith in him. "I have learned, though, in such times as these, that there is no other way."

"What you mean?" Alfred asked, shaking his head. He looked over at the American champion being carried off, leaving a thin line of blood. A hint of vomit bubbled in his throat. "If a hero not supposed to kill" He turned back to Mark, stiffening his chin, "then why there no other way?"

Two other champions were about to face off. Mark walked silently leading Alfred upon Nancy to the stables. Small torches flickered upon each of the support beams. The two brightest were above their stall.

"Do you remember the Dark Knight returning, and his fight with the clown I spoke of?"

Alfred nodded when the wizard lowered him to the ground. Tying Nancy off, Mark breathed deep before facing Alfred once again.

"He tried to kill him."

"What?" Alfred gaped. "You said the clown killed himself."

"True," Mark said, deciding to remove the horse's saddle. Alfred handed him the brush by the feeding bag before the wizard revealed the truth. "But to end things, the Dark Knight forced himself to act in a way he knew to be wrong. The clown was too dangerous to imprison again, for no cell could hold him. So, the Dark Knight tried, but the clown finished what he could not."

Minutes creaked by like the boards of the stands above them. A cracking shot through the rows of stalls until it was a whisper to their ears.

"Then I must kill father," Alfred sighed, "even if I know it wrong?"

"Precisely, or he will do so to you."

Taking the brush, Alfred smoothed the fur on the horse's flanks, continuing to the very base of its neck. The way the American boy's eyes had bulged and rolled shut made Alfred ponder the remaining boys he'd have to face. *They don't fear doin' it. But I want them to go free, not die.*

Setting the brush down, he looked wearily at Mark. Mark was wiping sand and sweat from the saddle with a rag, then eased it back in place.

"I'll kill father if I got to. I just afraid it may happen with the other boys."

"It shall prove difficult to be brave in these next few tilts. Be mindful that our father holds no remorse, unlike yourself and the others. I have seen boys fall to ruin from such an act."

Mark reached to reapply the saddle cinch, but Alfred did so instead. Mark thanked him with a pat on the back.

"I got to keep myself from fall then, I guess."

They walked under the stable's archway as a girl nearly as large as Maggie fell from her horse with a thud. She rolled to her feet, using the pitch to hoist herself up. She barked curses that Alfred knew were Swedish. Besides Italian and Swedish, there were four shelves on languages he had studied. One was marked "Languages of Europe." The shelf marked "Languages of Asia" was missing a few books, unlike the others.

Alfred translated for Mark, breaking up his depression like ice with a pick. Alfred laughed too, until the next jousters readied. One held a great helm in the shape of Horus the falcon-headed god, the other held a shield with a tower of crisscrossing beams affront a sunset. The tower champion taunted the Egyptian boy because of his missing nose.

When Charles threatened to have the wiry French boy hung for wasting time, the French boy laughed and said, "There is no tree here tall enough for me."

Charles leaned forward with another of his grins. "Who mentioned anything of trees?"

Alfred gulped as the French boy did when Charles motioned to the mountain's tallest point.

Both champions began soon after with the Egyptian boy seizing the moment of scattered nerves. The French boy, already too tall to ride a horse anyway, dug his heels into the sand at the same time the lance struck him.

Alfred gaped as the lance scraped across metal. The Egyptian boy laughed when his thrust sent his opponent spinning. And, with a wobble here and a wobble there, the French boy fell, hanging on the lists like a sheet of metal on a clothesline. The guards grabbed him, briefly forming a pair of iron clothespins. Soon after, all was set again for the next competitors. Alfred felt his heart thudding faster than before. A little boy with a velvet turban readied, his hands raised, to announce the Indian champion.

The thought of killing made Alfred's helmet feel like an oven. But when Emily planted herself in place of the boy, he remembered Maggie's words. She believed he could make things happen for himself. Taking the lance, Alfred stared point-blank at Charles for a split second, and then focused on the colors ahead. *Aim straight an' hard at his shield.* And then the two boys were off at a full gallop. Alfred made the first thrust, striking his opponent's shield.

What had been an elephant showered in flowers was now a gray smudge. Tiny splinters clung for seconds only to be shadowed by larger ones. A scream followed when a thin splinter pierced through the Indian boy's sandaled foot. Panic pinched Alfred's ears like the screams from the boy's lips. Alfred rode up next to him, only to be called back by Mark and shooed off by a colorfully dressed girl with a long, dark braid. He rode off, turning back to find the boy hold out his foot to the kneeling girl. She slid the thin splinter free, poured water on it, and then wrapped it.

Alfred was almost to his starting spot before a prayer, or what he thought was praying, drifted on the wind. This one was like a song, soothing his opponents nerves. Alfred said two prayers of his own before taking a lance. One for the boy and one for what he hoped would not happen. Charging, Alfred closed his eyes just as his thrust—

"*Crack*!" Familiar tremors burrowed tunnels through his arm. His lips and hands trembled. His eyes opened to find what he didn't expect. Just like the tremors now crawling, Alfred had anticipated too quickly. The Indian boy threw down his shield in disgust. The remains of its color had been scratched away, revealing the metal beneath. Cheers reached their pinnacle as Charles stood and raised his hands to announce the end of day one.

Back at Mark's, the excitement of his brothers and sisters quieted with the evening's passing. Alfred hugged his mother, finding it more rewarding than the children cheering his name hours earlier. The coming night wrapped itself around the mountain like her arms did him. This time, she didn't wipe her lipstick away when she kissed his cheek. He asked her about Leonardo, and when she said he would be okay, Alfred remembered the care she'd given him.

"I'm so proud of you, Alfred." Elsa gave him one final squeeze before making him a plate of dinner.

"We all are." Emily smiled while recording the day's triumphs.

In the firelight, her carefully written words mentioned nothing of what had happened to Maggie. He didn't mind. The image of Maggie being bathed in her father's blood was something he didn't want to read about later. Emily had shared the stories of their brothers and sisters. Every story had its own special title like, "Leonardo's Landing." She smiled at him when he whispered thank you. The longest tales were gruesome and hard to take, but Alfred knew she did not like to hide the past any more so than when Charles had taken her Beatles records. Nibbling on a carrot, Alfred remembered some of the worst he had read. He put their grim endings aside when Emily broke into song, and all began to clap.

The next day made last night's food and music a happy memory that Alfred wanted to see repeated. His nerves tingled when mounting his horse to face the boy of Japan. Breathing slowly to try and remain calm, the day was nearly over and only they remained. The boy slapped his bare hand against the rising sun on his breastplate. His hand reddened the more he did it. After the twelfth time Alfred wondered how he would hold a lance.

Slamming their visors shut, both boys charged forward. The Japanese boy, screaming at the top of his lungs, forced Alfred to resist the urge to cover his ears. The scream was so loud and angry it was as if someone had pressed a burning torch to the boy's tongue. "*Crack*" went two lances, littering the sand with splinters, the sound like a lightning strike. Alfred groaned, dropping his lance, whipping the reins until back at his starting point. His shield was bent inward. Mark eased the shield off, releasing Alfred's arm. The gauntlet was crushed, and his arm shook uncontrollably.

"There can be no doubt." Mark said. Alfred yanked his arm back just as Mark unfastened the gauntlet's last strap. "My apologies, Alfred," His eye were downcast, "but your arm is broken."

The squish of wet grass made them both look back to see Alfred's mother running from the stables. She slid his glove off slowly, making him bite his lower lip.

"You can't go on like this, my little knight," she said, biting back her emotions. "With no shield, you'll—"

"I'm not goin' to die, Mum." Alfred groaned. "Lot of kids need me. I—"

"No, you tried. And no one can ask any more." Elsa looked at his father. Alfred did too, seeing the satisfied look on Charles's face. "I'll settle this."

Alfred reached with his bad arm to stop her, only to pull it back in pain. She was within feet of the mountain lords when Charles rose. All was silent except for the mud sucking at Nancy's hooves. Mark seized her bridle before Alfred could spur her to aid his mother.

"She must face him." Mark rasped. "He has tormented her dreams for years, and—"

"You mean..."

Mark nodded as he began setting Alfred's arm. Alfred turned his head to block out the sight of the tightening cloth and wood. Doing so didn't hide what he hoped wasn't true.

"And what does my daughter wish to say, hmmm?" said Charles. "Does our son want to prove once again how unreliable he is, just like his mother?"

"No. We end this now. Free him, and"—she paused for a second, looking at Josephine— "my mother, and the others, and you can have me."

Alfred could not believe it. *Josephine's me grand mum.* Charles chuckled and leaned forward and met her eyes.

"I have had you once, and it gave me another I did not want." said Charles. Alfred's lips trembled when his father brought himself a breath of his mother. "I should think your nightmares would have made this offer an unwise one."

Alfred bit his lip to fend off the pain of one final tug of the cloth. His mother's hands shook like his, but her stance remained firm.

"No," Charles said, placing his hands on the railing. "He either keeps the bargain or Japan goes free."

Alfred knew he could not let his mother give herself up. He readied Nancy reins, drew in a breath, but before he could race to her side, Elsa climbed and slapped Charles. The sound carried into the ears of all, making many cringe and gasp.

"Let 'em all go!" she screamed.

"No, it's time I let you go."

It was a flicker—one so fast neither Alfred nor Josephine nor his mother had time to see it. His mother fell back when Charles recoiled. Alfred leapt from the horse, landing hard, running faster than he knew he could. His face was redder than his arm.

Collapsing to his knees, Alfred took her hand. The fall had taken its toll. Blood bubbled from her chest like it did from her lips. Her eyes struggled to stay open. He bent and kissed her forehead. The pain of his arm rose but was outmatch by what he felt in his heart.

Above, there were no smiles or laughter. Sobs from his grandmother turned to heavy breaths and dry heaves. Clenching his teeth, Alfred wished he had both arms to climb. But when he saw his father's face, there was no grin.

"She was supposed to be the key," Charles seethed. To Alfred, for once, he could read the one emotion he thought his father didn't have. Compassion. "All I desired was to end the line of so many failures. I had my chance, and what does breaking my own laws give me?" Alfred watched his father's finger tremble as he pointed. Both looked at his mother in those seconds, and in a rushed breath, his father finished. "Another failure like you."

His grandmother fled from the viewing stand in tears. Why the mountains? Why the tourneys? But the only question Alfred wanted answered was, "Why hurt someone you love?"

"What could an imbecile like you know of love?" Charles swallowed, rubbing his eyes. "It did not work with him."

Charles pointed to Mark when the wizard knelt to close Elsa's eyes. Mark's hands rested upon Alfred's shoulders as he spoke.

"It would have, Dad. If only you'd have given it a chance."

He an American? But the change did not matter. His mother was dead, and only one boy was left before he faced Charles. More than that, Alfred wanted to do the one thing he didn't wish to do ever again.

"When I win this, I'm not just goin' beat you, Father." Alfred swallowed. "I'm goin' to kill you."

"I highly doubt it, son."

Alfred watched Charles cleanse his face of emotion. He tried to pull his mother back to the stables, but his right arm wasn't enough. Then Mark took her left side and gave Alfred a nod as they pulled. Light, metallic footsteps came from behind, revealing the Japanese boy, who took her legs. His shallow cheeks and bony chin sunk deeper as he bowed his head in respect. The three struggled across the field, finding it slippery. One by one, other champions joined them when Alfred's feet pressed the sands of the lists.

Soon, his mother was high enough to make it to the stables. When all were at the Richards stall, they eased her down, each giving him a hug until only the Japanese boy remained.

"I'm sorry for your loss," he said. "It will bring great pain to my family for what I shall do, but..."

Alfred looked at him, knee-deep in straw, holding his mother's head in his lap. "If you're going to give me the match, I don't want you to."

"It would be an honor, for I know you shall free us all."

"Why you give up chance to be free? If I don't beat father..." Doubt wrapped itself around his heart like the cloth binding his splint.

The boy's bony fingers raised Alfred's chin. "No, my friend, do not fall into darkness, for I and others know you shall free us from it."

Alfred pulled his chin away, giving his mother one final hug and wiping his tears on the leather of his gloved hand. "And if father wins, then what?"

The champion of Japan placed his hands on Alfred's shoulders. A smile wrinkled his near-transparent skin as Alfred eased his mother's head to the straw to stand.

"Then at least hope was given by the truest Discarded Knight. Many believe that you shall win. *I* believe you shall win."

Alfred thought about it, remembering how he'd had to believe in himself to get this far, how others like his mother, Anna, Jacob, Maggie, Leonardo, Mark, and Emily had done so too. The sun's rays peeked through the stands, onto the boy. Alfred needed to believe again.

"Thank you. I will honor what ya did an' free us."

They gave one final look at his mother. A shuffle of feet met them at the archway. The mothers with the little ones who Alfred had seen just eleven days earlier hugged him. He thanked them as they went to watch over his mother. Across the arena, the rising sun banners still flapped, and the boy's horse shook its head.

"I will tell my family of my decision. I am sorry for what I have done to your arm. I hope it shall not impede your victory."

Shaking hands, both bowed to one another. Alfred looked across the sunbathed arena to those who stood within the shadows. And with his strength found, he went out to face his father.

Chapter 10

His arm was useless, and his fingers could barely close around the reins. The clouds drifted together again, turning the gold of his father's armor a bronze color. A throbbing ran into each of his teeth with every second Emily spent announcing him. He thought it was from fighting the pain in his arm, but this was different. It matched the stinging in his eyes, which had sprung up after telling his father to shut up.

Focusing on who sat ahead, he ignored the pricking at his lips. Charles slid on a helmet more ornate than the others. The Richards crest towered atop it made of solid gold. The stinging from before ran around Alfred's irises. He blinked, and tears welled from remembering the champion of Japan's forfeit.

The champion's father now loomed in the viewing stand, holding his son's sword. Red droplets fell onto the boy's body, which was hunched over below. Mark had told him that if any of the father's sons were to lose or surrender, they would be forced to kill themselves. A knife dug into the mud from the boy's stomach. Alfred turned away from him, ignoring the pooling blood the best he could, refocusing on his own father. The quick slash and roll of the boy's head and the words the boy's father said before the sword had fallen were hard to forget. *Defeat is shame, and forfeiting is a coward's excuse.*

Alfred gripped the familiar weight of what he hoped would be the last lance. This time it felt as though it had tripled. Without his other hand to balance, he could not help leaning heavily to the right. His visor was already shut, thanks to Mark. Rain pinged on his armor just as it had on the carriage's roof on the way to the asylum.

A trumpet sounded as father and son charged forward. The prick at his lips multiplied the more he clenched his teeth. The sting in his irises brightened across both eyes, filling the dark of his helmet. Through the grill of Charles's, Alfred could see that the same green. Aiming, Alfred blinked. Two cracks sent splinters flying, and Alfred leaning back, squeezing Nancy's sides tighter than the last time. Sitting up right as fast as he could, the Discarded cheered after he dropped the spent lance. Charles's shield was bent at the corner nearest his heart, and the blow had left a dent in his breastplate.

Alfred ignored the applause for what was only a tie. The hit had made him dizzy and confused at his strength. Taking a fresh lance, he looked up to see smoke billowing from Charles's helmet. His father grabbed his own lance so fast it knocked his squire down into a puddle with a splash.

Unhooking his red-hot visor, Charles flipped it open and yelled. "It won't matter if you win, Alfred!" He jammed his shield hand into a small pouch tied to his waist. Pulling his hand out, Charles held up a gold pocket watch. "There's no way any of those monsters will leave this world for the real one."

Alfred slid up his own visor. Pain ran from his fingers to his elbow. The rain tapped on Alfred's visor as Charles chuckled. When the zapping pain at his fingers eased, Alfred asked, "What a watch I broke got to do with freeing everybody?"

His father's laughter rose when a barrage of thunder sounded directly overhead, making all including Alfred jump a little.

"It has everything to do with it," said Charles, snickering, "thanks to your wish to play at knighthood."

Alfred remembered that day, leaving Gwen to have lunch. It was one of the few times Charles had ever been at home during the day. And with an arm waving a pencil like a sword, Alfred had knocked his father off balance onto the stairs. The fall had sent the watch down the third step as his father tried to catch himself. What came next, Alfred tried not to remember. He watched the rain envelop the pocket watch. Through the growing onslaught from above, its ticking was faint.

"You got it fixed?"

"How in the entire world can someone read so many works of fiction and fact and still be so indescribably dull?" Charles growled, narrowing his glowing eyes. "It's a time machine, and not even a bloody watchmaker can fix that. And with this time's primitive advancements, there is no way to use it again for its purpose."

A sly smirk from his father made all the Discarded turn toward him. Alfred wanted to climb into the pocket where the watch was placed again. Hissing and booing mixed with snarls from the Russian section returned Alfred to the memory of his short time at school. The boys forming their tightly layered circle with the Rosekuhs led by their eldest brother Roger.

For those seconds, he felt alone, the armor plating over his back drumming from the fingers crawling up it. Through all the noise, and the arena seeming to close in, he felt a hand rest on his leg. It was gentle like Jacob's on his shoulder when the three boys had been teasing him. He looked down to see, just like at school, that he was not alone.

"Make what you want to happen, happen, Alfred," Mark said. "We'll fix the watch just like you'll fix him."

For once taking a hint, Alfred slammed the visor shut, ignoring the pain, and jammed both spurs against Nancy's brown coat. Charles slammed his visor shut, cutting off the dark cloud his gloating had formed. Son and father readied with mere feet separating want and hate. Both sent green blasts from their eyes, forming into long, piercing lances, dwarfing those they aimed.

"*Crack.*" Light met light, exploding, making all turn away for an instant. Like the world around him, between the ticks of a second, Alfred did what no other man had done. He flew. A flicker, one he knew he could stop, went up just feet away—one his father reached to snatch away. Red droplets flew along with splinters as Charles fell back and Alfred fell forward. The rain blended with blood—but this time, Alfred neither gagged nor cringed. His fingertips slid across the watch's face, hiding minutes and hours. His bad arm tucked in and his good stretched as far as it could go.

Charles grabbed at his foot to pull him back only to curse him one final time.

Alfred landed, the sand splitting like a sword slicing through blackened flesh. The sand cushioned his fall, but the impact snapped his gorget's fasteners, ripping off his helmet. He grunted as grains of sand went into his shutting eyes.

Cheers rose up from the stands. He brushed sand from his prize. The watch was intact, but when Alfred turned to the lists, he gripped it tight. Charles lay atop it. His helmet was on the ground in pieces, and his face was in true form. A long, gold-scaled snout, eyes black as pitch with tiny green flashes slowly fading. Blood gushed up and over the gold of his breastplate. And like so many of his mother's stories, the dragon had been pierced through the heart.

Alfred kept his face still, hiding the suspicion that sprinted to tie the lead with his pulse. The green of his father's eyes were only tiny specks. The burning glow in his own eyes faded to normal only just before his father's went black. Emily, Mark, and Leonardo came running toward him.

"I fix 'em, didn't I?"

"You most certainly did," Mark said, returning to his wizardly speech, clapping Alfred on the back.

But when Alfred saw the look on Emily's face, her usual brightness was black—like their father's gaping, lifeless eyes.

"I guess this means we won't be seeing the Beatles. My mom had the best seats before..." She burst into tears.

Alfred knelt to comfort her. Panic rose from behind his father's seat, and the arena roared.

Leonardo knelt with him, realizing the same.

"Does this mean I won't see Momma back home in Rome?" Leonardo said.

The panic just fifty yards from them grew louder, making Alfred wish it hadn't. He wanted to comfort his brother and sister, but Japan and Russia's Discarded had seized the mountain lords. Some grabbed at the railing to escape, others swiped with needle-sharp claws, and some even tried to seize a hostage only to be overwhelmed.

Alfred moved toward them, keeping his face still while his mind ran from one thought to another. *They know something.*

There has to be a way to fix this. He looked at the watch. Its minute hand was trapped between a second and noon, yet for some reason, it still ticked.

One among the mountain lords kept his calm. He wore a white kilt with an ornate sash down the center and a headdress of blue and gold stripes. They met at the railing just as the champion of Japan's father had a knife pressed against his throat, making him drop the sword.

"I have observed you, boy. My mountain has some like you, but they are respected, and none carry my blood." The lord chuckled. "They are also quite amusing."

"I'm not here to make you laugh," Alfred said. "I know me father was probably lying to make me worry. You got to know how to fix it."

"My apologies for my own humor, and that of my king. I know none of you can take a joke." His face became still like the falcon of his champion's great helm. "With him out of the way, that will be of no bother. And you shall be put to work like my own blood."

Egypt's Discarded sat below delicately painted singular eyes upon white banners. The children were tan of skin, but dust layered them, making their long scars from every whiplash faint.

"That not gonna happen no more. You got a way to fix this or not?" Alfred squinted from the sun piercing the clouds, making the white behind the painted eyes almost invisible. "I kept the bargain and need one of you to—"

"Unfortunately,"—the mountain lord raised a hand to try and silence Alfred— "my king was correct in his words. This time does not allow a means to repair it, and he was its creator. So, any knowledge of its workings has, well, bled out."

Alfred looked back. Emily sat in Leonardo's lap as Mark tried to comfort them. At the lists, his father's face matched the color his armor had been earlier. Blood puddled below him on the sand.

"Then we don't need you, I guess."

The beastly Russian children roared, and the Japanese drew long, black, pointed knives. All were ready to end the panicking lords. The one of Egypt fell to his knees. A hint of gold formed in his eyes as they turned to true form.

"Wait," he growled, struggling to stand when blades pressed against his scaly stomach. "You must not be cruel the way we have."

"And why should we not be?" Mark yelled. He had moved beside Alfred, who was ready to say the same. "You have worked us, bled us, and have used this tourney for your own amusement."

The black scales and white teeth of the Egyptian's father slowly turned human again. The mountain lord hid his fear as Alfred asked Mark if anyone had found Josephine. But the wizard shook his head, saying that she was neither atop the mountain nor anywhere else. The castle was sealed shut.

She may be in there.

"Let him speak!" Alfred yelled when steel was ready to cut through flesh. "Tell us. I want to know."

Images of his mother, Maggie, the Thai boy, and the Japanese boy who'd forfeited knowing its cost, filled Alfred's head. Alfred raised his hand, ready to drop it if what was said didn't truly matter. His wish to not kill was waning.

"Each of us had our reasoning for imprisoning our children. Some did so out of perfection, others for sheer amusement, but I and my Incan brother did it because of what we knew the world would become."

"And what would it?"

"I think I know what he speaks of, Alfred," Mark said. "And though it is noble to protect what remains of old civilizations, it does not pardon the millions who have died in this one—" The wizard's words caught in his throat. Rampant coughing squeezed at his lungs, sending him to his knees.

Alfred tried relaxing his brother by patting his back. His worry for Mark fought against those who seethed high above him. The Egyptian father stared at them, as did the children holding still a millennium—or more—worth of anger.

"I'm sorry, Alfred. But we must not permit them to live. "We –" Mark coughed again, sending red droplets onto the drying grass.

Alfred's face whitened. His little legs shook. His brother and mentor was truly sick. He could not understand why Mark wasn't like the others. To make it all worse, Alfred had to decide if those with good or cruel intentions deserved to live. He looked at the watch, and then at the frightened mountain lords, and then at Mark. *Make what you want to happen, happen.* Mark's words ticked in his mind like the watch in his hand and the pain in his splinted arm. He held the watch tight, and then he remembered something.

"Let them go," he said. "I—"

Hundreds of threats and curses rang out from what had been silence.

"I have not seen my mother in so long," said a boy.

"For all we know, our mothers are dead." said a girl. She shook her fist below the cress crossed tower banner of France. "We should kill them and you and burn their palaces."

Alfred wanted to say what he remembered, and tell them that it would solve everything, but the cries became too numerous. The noise made him want to run out of the arena, to cut through the fields beyond until reaching the water's edge. He couldn't swim the channel separating him from the mountain villages of Europe. The pressure was crashing like the clear, blue waters Mark had spoken of. Alfred wanted to jump in and let the waves carry him away. Except that would be just what his father and the lords wanted. To leave would mean to forget them all just like the world had.

"You going to return whenever you came from. I will bring you home."

Whispers buzzed in place of curses or more threats. What he remembered was the last book he had ever read. It had sat upon the toppled pile of books the day he asked Charles to let him attend school. Throughout its margins were scribbles of what he recognized now to be the watches inner workings. The images and instructions replayed in his head when the Egyptian mountain lord spoke again.

"You must be hard of hearing. Your father said there is no way to repair it, especially within a century able only to make that thing tell time once more. And only he knows its workings."

"So, what shall it be, boy?" A gulp and a stiff chin replaced the fear in the Japanese lord's trembling face. "Death to us, or—"

"No one is going to die." said Alfred, looking at Mark, who was as confused as the others, but his coughing had stopped. "I know how to fix it, and it don't take much."

More whispers ran up and down each row and section as he rested the watch's face gently on his broken arm. Alfred searched for the smallest and strongest of splinters he could find, kicking sand over the bigger ones. Something round and shiny peeked among the remnants of his father's helmet. Recognizing the small screw from his own helmet, he used its point to remove the watch's back.

All watched and waited. The light from the watch turned Alfred's lips blue. Sweat ran down his face as he gently twisted, pressed, and slid its inner workings. The tension was high. He knew those holding back their anger were growing impatient. When he'd done what he could, one thing above all else could not be fixed and needed replaced.

"The memory is dead, an' there is no way to replace it."

"What do you mean by memory?" Emily asked.

"He means whatever kept our times on record is of no use," Mark said.

Alfred didn't have to look up to know that the Discarded's whispered excitement had silenced. He knew, as Mark somehow did, that all were stuck here without precise years, dates, and locations.

"Wait, I know what we can do," Emily said. "It's so groovy, you'll buy me a milkshake when I show you the sixties."

All looked at Emily when she plopped her satchel in front of her. She pulled out a leather-bound book, holding it high with a smile and giggling. Alfred's eyes lit up, along with Mark's, when she read aloud the first location.

"March 9, 1964, London, England is—"

Cheers rose up before she could finish. Leonardo jumped up and down, lifting her onto his shoulders. The Egyptian father looked around as the other lords did. Instead of being afraid or angry, his lips trembled.

"And what will become of my children? I brought them from every near collapse of Egypt there was, and the last ended the pharaohs. They have a purpose in building my monuments. In the past, they faced extinction—"

"You whip 'em and starve 'em. That don't sound like saving to me," Alfred said. He was still smiling from Emily's idea, but the mountain lord's words made sense. "I don't want bad stuff to happen to none of 'em, but..."

The more Alfred thought about it, the more he remembered what had happened when he'd been finally freed of his home. People were cruel. The world smelled and was loud. And in the end, each of them would have to grow up. *But it's better than staying here. They can't have adventures or fall in...* A tear ran down his cheek when he looked over at the cage where his father had left Maggie. He had loved everything about her. She'd made him laugh, and he'd made her smile. Now she was gone, not allowed to grow up or prove herself, or ride the horses her father trained. *Or be with me...*

"I guess they just gon' to have to face what es coming."

He adjusted the watch's bezel as the mountain lords and their children waited. The watch's face lit up, growing brighter, forcing Alfred's eyes shut. Its light cooked him in his armor, so he pointed it toward the wall below the mountain lords. An immense, churning portal appeared instantly, turning blue and white. From a hole where the chain had been, numbers and words projected. Squinting, Alfred tapped the numbers mentioned in his father's notes. Beside each scribble was a date that looked important. *December 31, 6189007.*

"No!" The Egyptian father shouted. He morphed into a large, black-scaled dragon. His eyes glowed gold. His swipes sent his captors running. The other lords tried the same but were held down by knifepoint. "That is the end of all time."

The lord leapt to the ground, ready to attack. A large shadow grabbed his hands.

"Leave my brother be. You be going back." Leonardo grunted as he struggled to hold the lord back.

Alfred quickly typed in a random location. *Antarctica.*

"No, you shall doom us! Unhand me, you behemoth."

"Momma says you just have to live life, and things be okay."

The lord roared louder as the strain gripped at Leonardo's legs. Mark urged the Discarded to throw the lords into the portal. The lords followed the Egyptian's lead, biting and clawing. With a roar louder than the rest, the Russian champion appeared from the stairs behind them, but not alone.

"Alfred!" Josephine yelled, peering from behind the towering Russian.

Alfred smiled when Josephine ran to the railing, doing so even wider when her protector punched and pushed the lords away. Japan's sons and daughters did the same, forcing the lords to the railing.

Loud thuds sent grass and mud everywhere. Alfred watched helplessly as Leonardo pushed hard, struggling to replant his feet. The Egyptian lord ripped his arm away, slashing at the giant's stomach, taking cloth and flesh.

"No!" Alfred yelled, but Leonardo kept pushing through his bellowing tears.

The black dragon swiped again, only to have the artistic giant catch his hand. Blood dripped between his brother's legs as Alfred held steady his tears—just like he held the watch. The time portal held strong, swallowing each lord, and then burping snowflakes.

"You are worse than your father if you send us to the cold," The Egyptian mountain lord cried. "There is nothing left there but ice and the souls you send toward it."

A warning flashed on the holographic projection, one Alfred hoped wasn't true. *Warning: Earth's final date is a frozen wasteland. Continued portal use will carry its fate to the past.*

"Hurry, Leonardo!" Mark and Alfred yelled.

"I try, but—uuh!" Leonardo stumbled. The blasts of cold made it worse, and his wound was leaving puddles instead of droplets.

"Somebody got to help him," Alfred said. "I have to keep the watch going."

The cold air gave shape to his breath as the muddy grass froze. The Discarded held each other close for warmth while the black dragon snapped at Leonardo's neck. Alfred wished he could use the strength he'd shown earlier. The watch's warning flashed again. Hands clasped over Alfred's, and he saw Mark's shadow.

"Help our brother, Alfred."

"But you don't know how—"

"Do it! I shall explain when that monster is black ice."

Alfred ran to help Leonardo, howling artic winds muffling the coughing fits behind him. Alfred saw his brother's knees give and arms shake. Alfred's eyes glowed as he came closer. The remaining mountain lord cackled when Leonardo gave in. Leonardo fell back, hitting the ground as Alfred's teeth sharpened. With one hand, Alfred grabbed the lord by the leg. A thud accompanied by a growl sent ice crystals upward. The lord swiped at Alfred, but like Albert had said, Alfred was small and hard to hit.

"Let go. I am your king now." The mountain lord swiped again, but Alfred dodged it. "What shall pathetic creatures like you do without one to rule?"

Pulling with his discovered strength, Alfred almost had him to the portal. The gold of his scales felt the needle pricks of the wind. He stared at his captive's panicking gold eyes, wanting almost to spare him. His good arm ached with each tug and pull. Another warning sounded, increasing the snow and ice, and slowing his movement. If anyone should lead—not rule—the Discarded, it shouldn't be one who wanted to enslave them.

"I'm sorry, but you don' deserve to be king."

The lord narrowed both eyes, but they bulged from another blast of cold. The look on the black dragon's face made Alfred again the little knight his mother loved. With a heave, he flung the mountain lord into the portal just as his claws made one final swipe. Mark closed the portal, sending a rush of flakes across the arena. The Discarded ran from their seats before it all turned to icicles, shattering on the worn bleachers.

The arena's center looked like a frozen road leading to the mountain above. The Discarded gathered on what was still green and brown. None of the immense armored guards stopped them. Instead, the steel-clad giants fled from the arena into the trees south of it. Emily hugged Alfred. His scales slowly faded to skin and his eyes phased to their dark green.

They moved with all the others to Leonardo as he lay with reddened hands on his stomach. The bright blues, greens, purples, and oranges of his tunic looked black under the blood. Leonardo's heavy, quick breaths made Alfred wish he knew more of medicine. He had never read any books on how to heal someone. All were silent as Mark handed him the watch.

"I'm afraid I can't help him either," he said, reluctantly returning to his American accent. "I only know how to set an arm. And this—well, he has lost too much blood for me to try anything."

"It is fine," Leonardo groaned. The fading giant coughed. "I shall miss my momma now more than ever, but at least I be free."

Footsteps followed the tears of the Discarded. Alfred turned to see Josephine by his side. She knelt and hugged him. He wanted more than any of his other brothers and sisters to see Leonardo returned home. The giant had been one of the few to live so long in the mountain's jaws. He stroked Leonardo's face with his bad hand, ignoring the pain. Little by little, Leonardo's eyes struggled to stay open.

"Thank you, my piccolo brother."

"*Prego*, Leonardo."

Alfred rested his head on his grandmother's shoulder. Slowly, his brother's eyes rested shut. The rise and fall of Leonardo's stomach sank one final time. Closing his eyes, Alfred prayed harder than he had ever done. He did so silently, keeping the words even from his ever-racing mind's eye. All around, prayers in every language he knew—and in some he had yet to master—were said.

When they finished, Emily still held her book. Its thickness made him hope that the remaining Discarded had kept such records. None had, not even Egypt's. A people who were renowned for keeping good records in stone and on papyrus. Running his fingers across the book's worn leather, he leafed through it, finding each page filled from top to bottom.

"I don't know what to do, Mark," Alfred said. "Our brothers an' sisters can go home, but none of 'em can."

"I understand, and I wish now that I was a real wizard." Mark stifled another coughing fit.

"How you sick after bein' here so long?"

"Alfred, I do not believe this may be the—" Josephine said.

"It's okay," said Mark.

Alfred breathed easy once Mark assured his grandmother, he'd known the question was coming. Mark scanned the crowd, spiking Alfred's worry again. His brother's face was turning red.

"I guess when Dad sent me here, the fact that I was already old somehow dulled this world's magic." Mark ceased what looked to be counting. "Our mountain village will hold them. Without their dads, they can't go back to their villages. Do you remember the calculations on the cell wall?"

Alfred nodded, wishing he had paid more attention to math just as he wished their father's study had had books on medicine.

"I found the watch when we lived in Pittsburgh. Dad found out when we went to his London butcher shop. I had no idea it would land me in an asylum. Plus, I was the one who wrote in that book."

Alfred's jaw dropped. "Then you can fix de watches memory?"

"That's not quite how it works." Mark shivered, just as Alfred did. The portal had made the autumn air colder even though it was closed. "This is future tech, and it isn't like putting a candle in the window on a cold, dark winter's night."

The reference to the song Mark had sung last night made Alfred grin a little despite the bombardment of bad news. Many of the older Discarded agreed with Mark, but when Emily heard the news, she hugged Alfred again.

"I don't want to go home if no one else can. I'd sell my Beatles tickets if that would help." She sniffed back her tears, sliding two tickets from her satchel's outer pocket. Both looked as good as the day her mother had bought them. "I wish it would."

"Me too, Emily." Alfred flipped through the book, finding the smithies' locations. "I'm gonna send me brothers and sisters' home, everybody." Readying the watch, he paused before entering the location. "Does any of you want to go with 'em?"

No one stepped forward, and none spoke of how unfair it was. Alfred thought about what he had decided earlier, knowing the idea he was forming was a risky one. The smithies walked through one by one. Christopher saw the sadness in Alfred's eyes. Alfred smiled when the helpful boy was halfway through his welcoming. Robert snatched him by the collar once it began again, then gave Alfred a wink and a thanks just as Albert had done.

Many more portals opened and closed, some filled with sounds. Alfred wondered who or what may be making them. The last boy to leave wore the demon shirt and sang a song that Mark said was from a band called Styx. Alfred loved the title, "I Want to Know What Love Is." With the final line, the boy bowed into the eighties. The Discarded clapped louder than ever this time. Though he was still sad like Emily and Mark, the applause was better spent on something beautiful rather than bloody.

A few days and tears passed. Alfred led the Discarded west toward the ocean. Mark had suggested the spot for its high, white cliffs and said that the west meant freedom. By then, Alfred was able to flex his fingers more. When Mark had removed the splints the night before, they'd decided they would lead the Discarded with Emily and Josephine's help.

The high green grass brushed against Alfred's hips. The Russian Discarded had lowered Maggie and her father in front of their obelisks. His mother was brought last, being aligned with a third obelisk, which bore her name like the others. The children of Egypt's Discarded had suggested them, wishing Alfred could have used the same resins to preserve them like those of their faraway home.

When all were gathered upon the grassy hill before the high cliffs, Mark requested a moment of silence. It broke once the wind blew a cold draft against their backs. The chill made the youngest want to leave in a hurry. The cold reminded Alfred of the day he'd climbed down the mountain. He hugged his grandmother for a moment, then they knelt beside his mother. The hole from the knife had been sewn and the blood had been washed clean. Alfred brushed back a single hair trying to escape from the bun Josephine had done upon her daughter's head. They kissed Elsa on the cheek after a long prayer. Alfred remained on his knees, tears running down his cheeks, dripping into the ocean of grass.

"I may not have been with you for most of me life, but I—" His face shook, turning red. His tears struggled in the wind with the words on his lips. "I loved you the whole time I was blamin' me self for you being gone. And then I finally got you back. Even in them brief days, it made it all better. I'm happy to have known you for that long."

Josephine hugged him, kissing his cheek. "That was the kindest thing a son could ever say. She would be proud of you, as I am."

"Thank you."

Rubbing his eyes, Alfred wanted to say the same to Maggie, but knew, if anything, that she was happy. Her father and she would be on horseback in what would be endless fields to roam. And maybe when his time came, Alfred could ride alongside them.

For now, he watched patiently as each was lowered on a makeshift raft into the foaming waters below. The waves crashed against the cliffs, their foam sizzling. Alfred hoped, with the clouds forming overhead, that the current would carry them safely west.

Once they were well enough out to sea, Alfred walked with his grandmother, brother, and sister to their mountain. Its vast gray teeth and scale-like sides were hidden by thick clouds of smoke. The night before, Alfred had the arena and castle burned. Many of the Discarded had danced and sang the songs of what they could remember of their own times. The four were silent for some time until one question that until now had never been important enough was asked.

"Mark?"

"Yes, Alfred?"

"How you learn to talk the way you did?"

Mark laughed and gave Alfred a pat on the shoulder. "If one must be a wizard, one must speak like the best in all of literature."

"And who is the best?" Emily giggled.

Giving a smile and a wink, Mark told the story of a wizard in gray, and another small in stature who wielded a magic ring. It was one Alfred could relate to, a story he would always remember and never have to read.

About the Author

Andrew Johnston is a fantasy writer from southwestern Pennsylvania with an imagination stretching beyond the borders of his hometown. He is the author of the Iron Frost Universe series. Andrew studies history and spends time with his nephew when not writing.